Adventures

by

Lee Keith Freeman

ISBN 9798697880647

BeliefNexus.WordPress.com

Adventures in Space & Time

(Freeman's Fable Volume II)

Or

Marmalade's Marvelous Misadventures with Tinker the Time-Travelling Tabby

(This title seemed a bit too long though, hence the shorter one. Oh and it's the 2nd part of Freeman's Fables, but I think you knew that as you got this far in the book, and you're not a complete idiot. Unlike some people.)

Written by Messrs'

Lee Keith Freeman

&

Marmalade

++Top Secret ++++++++++**Classified Document**++++++++Confidential++

This document contains classified information - The contents within should only be revealed to relevant staff with Level 1 clearance - For Their Eyes Only - Only For You - You Will See What No One Else Can See And Now I Am Breaking Free - For Their Eyes Only - Ooo Ooo Ooo Ooo - Enough of this nonsense - Please redact copy if copied - If not then it is alright - That is okay dude - Do not send electronically - Do not send by post - Only hand it to people you know, that includes Eric from the spa and gym, MachoFit - He is an agent you see - Does dead-drops for favours - In no way give it to Fitz, he is a Russian double agent - Mary is alright though - But even so, this is Top Secret - Confidential - Classified - For Your Eyes Only.

Operational Mission Details: Unplugged Feline

Name: Marmalade
Codename: Robinsons
Species: Cat
Age: Unknown

Name: Tinker
Codename: Tailor
Species: Cat
Age: 22 cat years

Objective: Traverse Space-Time and observe historic moments – Check to see if foreign intelligence is using Time Travel to copy space flight information & technology, or stealing covert intelligence via use of time/space navigation so to promote and advance their own technology.

Field Notes: In the early 1960s it became apparent that CIA Project Acoustic Kitty had been an absolute failure. As a result, Operation Unplugged Feline was given the go ahead and two reasonably trained cats had communicative-translator earphone, microphone and speaker features installed. Agents Tailor & Robinsons then successfully built a time travel device. The head engineer was Tailor. After a successful test run, the two cats pursued navigation of space-time with partial success. Ultimately, the time travel device was successful. The current whereabouts of the vehicle is unknown. The current whereabouts of the cats is also unknown. Status of their progress: Transient. The ultimate result of the operational success is on a need to know basis. So if you need to know, then you would know what we know and if you don't know, then you don't need to know what we know. What we do know is known only to the few on the need to know basis and what is unknown is known by everyone, including myself, but we don't know what we don't know and if we did know what we don't know, then we'd all be a little wiser. It is believed that the cat agents Tailor & Robinsons went underground and are currently carrying out a Black Ops mission somewhere near Welwyn Garden City, UK. They have not gone rogue but they have gone further undercover to find out what we all don't know, so we will eventually know what is to be known. This much is known - that they encountered some form of alien life, an entity, and as a result had to lay low. We also know that wherever there is trouble, if you need help, and if you can contact them or find them, they will help you.

Current Status: In Progress.

The feline version of the beginning of everything,

According to Ezra the Ancient, Year 0, Just after 3PM

In the beginning, the Supreme Cosmic Being looked around and saw it was empty. There was so much space, so the Supreme Cosmic Being got some cans and for the cans there came forth hands, and these hands opened the cans that filled the vast expanse. Everything came forth from the cans; elements, atoms, stars, planets, meat, cheesy Cheeky Chunks, milk, spaghetti hoops, beans, cat-food, lentils, light aircraft, sofas, chairs, pillow stuffing, lint, those lace placemat things that really have no purpose other than looking nice on an occasional table, catnip, little balls with bells in that rattle around when chased, lamps and time, moreover all things we know came forth from the cans, held by the hands in the vast expanse. Then the Supreme Cosmic Being, saw it was looking pretty good and thought, "Yeah dude, I like it."

Then in the corner of the cosmos, a little galaxy had a planet floating about the place and the Supreme Being thought, "That'll be a good place to start something different." So the Being planted some trees and plants, then created lots of living things; humans, doglings, helefumps, dwarves, giraffes, flies, spiders, moths, flutterflies and, of course, us catlets. They were told to go forth and multiply, so they did. Then the Supreme Cosmic Being placed humans in charge, but called a catlet over so an information could be conveyed.

"I've placed the human doings in charge, but keep an eye on them please, if it's not too much trouble. I'm not sure I was wise to let them be in charge of this planet, so I need faithful catlet custodians to oversee them. Can you do this, dude?" said the Supreme Being. And that catlet said, "Yeah sure, no sweat, dude, that's coolio."

Then certain perturbation happened, something to do with a garden and a tree with fruit, which opened up a whole new can, of worms this time, and everyone got moved out of this super, deluxe, walled type garden thing, which was kinda upsetting, as we all liked it in there. So people moved about, animals migrated about the place and a thing called belief started. Where people settled, they had their own ideas about Cosmic Being, but when people started fighting and wars happened, ideas came together to form new ideas about religion, so lots of beliefs started to pop up, all improving on the ones before them. So us catlets kept some continuity by recognizing the Supreme Cosmic Being and kept an eye over the human dudes. At first it was a bit obvious, due to the Egyptian's so we had to say, "Stop worshipping us catlets, dudes. Worship the one we call upon, not us!"

So us catlets moved to more obscure realms, watching from a distance, making sure those humans didn't foul up again, like in the walled garden type thing. Faithfully and dutifully we serve the Supreme Cosmic Being, for this is our privilege and duty.[1]

---

1 Parenthetically, this was translated by me, Marmalade. Well, who else is going to do it? The author? He's an absolute idiot. No, I wrote this bit but the author had to put his two pence worth in. Anyway, on with the book...

Newbottle, Tuesday 31st August 2020, 1803hrs

"I've only gone and cracked it, ain't I?"

An unamused feline looked up momentarily then resumed its activity, saying, "That should be, 'haven't I.' What has five letters: is not dissonant, musically, yet like a Mandarin or Cantonese – last letter is an L?"

"Dunno. I've done it! I've done it!"

"Your vocabulary, dear boy, is absolutely atrocious! However, I am now inclined to ask, what have you discovered?"

A grey and black, tabby cat excitedly jumped about, making the other cat pause his crossword conundrum.

"I, my friend, have cracked time travel."

The marmalade coloured, Persian puss raised its eyebrows.

"So, the enigma that's eluded humankind for eons has been solved by a cat? Hmm. Yet, you don't know what has five letters: is not dissonant, musically, yet like a Mandarin or Cantonese – last letter is an L, correct?"

"Yeah."

"And how, pray tell, have you discovered the ability to traverse through time?"

"I've created a device that opens a portal through which space-time folds and takes me to another moment in time."

"How exactly? By eating jelly doughnuts? Scratching cat litter in a reverse formation?"

"No," said Tinker. "By subverting the singularity and extrapolating a formula based on this, I created a device based on time-space relations where the fenestration of time is like a series of tangents that are theoretical passages through time, like a mole digging through the earth."

"You mean, you've created a wormhole?"

"No, I can create portals with this..."

A twisted tin can containing something that rattled, lay on the floor. Several yellow and blue lights sporadically lit up and a sudden beep, surprised both cats.
"What, that thing?"
"That 'thing' is a quantum-flux modulator, with Einstein-Rosen qualities that bridges two moments in time together. It warps conventional space-time causing a gravitational effect on assorted quanta, to produce a tunnel warped by negative energy rotating in and out of existence, yet is finely balanced by a compensation of Heisenberg-enhanced leptons, so a static warp shell can be traversed safely by living beings, chiefly cats."
"Yet you still don't know what has five letters: is not dissonant, musically, yet like a Mandarin or Cantonese – last letter is an L."
"Forget the chuffin' crossword, man. Come here and try it..."

Marmalade walked over to the tin can and tabby. Looking down upon the contraption he kicked it.
"Don't do that!"
"Ok clever clogs; take me to see Napoleon just before he became an arrogant arse."
"One momento, paw favor... X=3m squared by xp times 19 co-sine, bish, bash bosh."

The two cats suddenly disappeared, then briefly reappeared, only to reappear fully a second later.
"Tinker, you're a bloomin' idiot! That wasn't Bonaparte, that was Napoleon the second! I want to see the first part, not the sequel! Hang on... I think, you.... I think... You've done it, Tinker! You've actually, chuffin' done it!"

Marmalade was astounded and lost for words. Striding around the tin can contraption, he spied the very thing that now enabled cats to travel through time.
"Never in a million years would have I said that you,

Tinker, would solve the problem of time travel! Yet you have."
"See, I told you; I done it."
"No, it's, 'I did it."
"No, I found it."
"Yes, I know."
"But you said, you'd done it."
"No, I said, 'I did it."
"But I have found it,"
"I know you have... look this is getting us nowhere! Suffice to say, you are a bloomin' genius. Come, let us partake in a journey of adventure, leading us through perilous trajectories to all ports of time in this veritable multiverse."
"Dunno, 'bout that, but I'm goin' time hopping, mate."
"Wait, I must pack my water bowl and cat-statins, as I have terribly high kitty cholesterol."
"Where shall we go?"
"Take your pick, dude, your choice first."
Tinker thought for a while, then programmed the device, watching the lights blink and the LED display whirl a flurry of numbers.
"Where are we going?"
"Follow me, Marmalade, were going somewhere amazing..."
"To get an answer to the crossword puzzle?"
"No, somewhere even better..."
Then both cats suddenly disappeared.

Sand blew in their faces and the heat immediately poured its warmth on to them.
"Boy, it's hot! So hot," said Tinker.
"You're hot! How do you think I feel? I've got twice as much hair as you, dude! Anyway, where are we?"

"Dunno."

The cats looked around at the surroundings, noticing the heat haze rise off the ground. In the distance some feint shapes could be seen.

"Over there, Tinker. We'll head that way, to the building site. Looks like there's a nice garden near there too."

So the cat explorers ventured over to what looked like a building site next to a walled garden. In the distance, someone could be seen running towards them gaining ground every second. As the stranger neared, Marmalade tried getting the person's attention.

"Hello, I'm wondering if you can possibly help me; how far away is Pontefract from here? Hello?"

The man raced past hurriedly, saying something unintelligible, as he pursued his course. Some men, looking like a small posse, chased after him. As they neared, Marmalade tried addressing them.

"Excuse me, could you kindly advise if we are near Northallerton? These are different environs that I'm used to and I wonder if this is indeed Northallerton?"

One of the posse stopped for a moment and questioned Marmalade in an unfamiliar tongue.

"I'm sorry, I don't understand your dialect. Try saying it a little slower."

The stranger repeated his question.

"I'm sorry, don't you speak English? I can't make head nor tail of the gibberish you're saying. Let's try something else; do you know what has five letters: is not dissonant, musically, yet like a Mandarin or Cantonese – last letter is an L?"

The man shook his hand at the cats, exclaimed something then rushed off to join his band of pursuants.

"Tinker, where are we?"

"Not sure, one moment..."

"It seems like a desolate, sandy wasteland."
"Could be Ilkley Moor..."
"Well, that's certainly desolate, but what's with the sand? Has someone turned it into a litter box?"

Tinker finished analyzing the tin can and said, "We're in Mesopotamia. Where's that?"
"Oh, so we're down south then, somewhere near Littlehampton I believe. What year are we in?"
"Not entirely sure, but around 2659 BC, give or take a decade."
"Uhm. I feel your device needs a little refinement. Maybe also consider inventing a translation machine so we can understand what on earth people are saying and vice versa."
"Right. Ok, hang on..."

In a trice, the cats were back in their own time, in the living room of the house where they lived.
"How did we get home to this exact location?"
"I fixed a translocation buoy in the space-time of our residence so we can ferry about safely."
"That was a good idea! What made you think of doing that?"
"Well, I knew that those reading this book would wonder how we would get back home so easily."
"What very good forward thinking of you."
"Truth be told, it wasn't me but the author."
"Oh, right, that idiot."

Tinker at once began to figure a way of creating a translator device so language could be understood between humans and animals, as well as from one language to another. Remembering his past, he had an idea and began programming the tin can.
"I think I can solve the language problem thingy by contacting a colleague in the CIA."

"The CIA? When were you in the Central Intelligence Agency?"

"During the Cold War. I was recruited as one of 5 cats to be a surveillance operative in Project Acoustic Kitty. They hardwired equipment into our ears and skull to receive and transmit information we heard whilst walking about in parks."

Then in an instant, Tinker disappeared with Marmalade, taking them to Langley, Virginia in 1960s America. Padding through the corridors, they searched for the laboratory where Tinker had been trained. Room 2523 was eventually found and after bypassing the security measures, by sneaking in when a human entered, they approached a large Burmese cat who was testing some equipment.

"Howdy, Tinker. How yer doin' bro?"

"You know that surveillance stuff they integrated into our anatomy for Acoustic Kitty? Well, I need to adapt it to become a universal translator, so me and my friend here can understand other tongues."

"Yes," said Marmalade. "And I also wonder if you can answer a question for me?"

"How to join the CIA?" asked the Burmese.

"No; what has five letters: is not dissonant, musically, yet like a Mandarin or Cantonese – last letter is an L?"

"Ain't no Idea, bro, but I can help with translator aspect. We've been working on this, a translingual implant that converts sound to information the feline brain can discern as logical syntax for communication purposes. If I tweak it to work with a microphone, I can probably do what you're asking for; give me a moment..."

The Burmese toddled off with his ideas ensconced in his head. A while later, a scientist came in with some food for the cats, that actually was laced with a sedative, which sent both of them to sleep.

A few minutes passed and they awoke in a cage somewhere in CIA headquarters. Feeling drowsy, they attempted to stir and make sense of what was happening to them.

"Dammit! We've been drugged," exclaimed Tinker.

"No kidding, Sherlock! You imbecile! How are we going to get out now, eh?"

The Burmese approached and made to undo the cage latch, apologising for the human's tactics. The chloroformed cats, slid out of the cage and tried to stand up, but failed miserably so lay back down.

"You've been in surgery. Both of you now have a microphone in your jaw, earphone in your ears and a speaker in your neck to help filter sound-waves. You can hear and speak in virtually any language now, thanks to our linguistic technology, except the Welsh language, as frankly, we ain't a clue what those guys are talking about."

"I see," said Marmalade. "I'm not used to being a covert operative: is there anything I need to be aware of in particular?"

"Nope. Just avoid water, as it shorts the circuitry."

"Thanks, Billy," said Tinker as he high-fived the Burmese, then guided Marmalade to the door, so they could return to where the tin can time machine lay and return home.

"Well, that was most fortuitous, wasn't it, Tinker?"

"Yes. I hope we have cause to use this technology, otherwise it would be a waste of a section of this story!"

"Hmm. Absolutely. Now, young Tinker, let us traverse time with our tin can and appropriate translation hardware, in the hope of having some exciting adventures!"

"Yes, I do hope we get to use this equipment to advance our knowledge and understanding of things."

"Yes, and also solve the conundrum of my crossword clue. Come, Tinker, let us go boldly to where no cat has been before...!"

Then Marmalade began singing a theme song to a popular television show, but rather badly.

On a mountain somewhere near Tahiti, 3rd March 2020, sometime after lunch

On the precipice of a mountain, up in the range, lay a small pile of rubble. It was a dreary, dull, cloudy day and the rain was looming on the mountain tops, gathering momentum and getting ready to pour. As it got closer, one smallish stone sensed a lack of stability and was bracing itself, ready for the downpour. Then just as the first drop hit the top of the stone, a tremendous clash of thunder sounded. Feeling even more unsteady, the sound eventually moved the stone so it began to tumble down the mountainside. Down and down it went, bouncing and banging against the mountain's edge. Other rocks and stones followed close by, until they hit a body of water.

Along the water it was pushed by the gathering swell and with the water on top, the stone was forcibly pushed along the floor of the river. For miles and miles along the floor the small stone went, pushed by the weighty waters. The crescendo began to subside and the roar of the event became quieter, meaning the stone gradually came to standstill. Gently ending its journey, it rocked into a suitable spot and gathered itself together.

"What on earth is happening now? What's with all the raucous noise? Is there any need to be thrown here in such an abrupt manner?"

"Here, we go; we got another one," said the limpet who lingered nearby.

"I was resting, quite nicely, up in my mountain, y'know, just chillin' with me mates, when this bloomin' great clap of thunder knocks me off the edge and I get thrown down in to the water. And then I get thrown about until I get to this, this, this..."

"Ocean?" asked the limpet.

"I'm gonna complain."

"And whom are you going to complain to?"

"Get me the manager!"

"There is no manager."
"Then get me the boss, the foreman, the chairman... whoever!"
"It won't get you anywhere."
"I don't care! Get me the person I can complain to, now."
A lowly turtle wandered over and looked at the stone.
"What's wrong?" said the turtle.
"I was resting, quite nicely, up in my mountain, y'know, just chillin' with me mates, when this bloomin' great clap of thunder knocks me off the edge and I get thrown down in to the water. And then I get thrown about until I get to ocean."
"And?"
"Well, I'm not happy about it!"
"Uhm. What we have here is something known as a stalemate."
"What are you on about? I'm complaining – I'm not stale, mate!"
"Well, let me explain this to you, as simply as I possibly can through three salient points that may have eluded you: one, no one is going to be able to put you back up on the mountain. Two, complaining is going to solve absolutely nothing. And three, no one cares that another bit of rock is down here, in this ocean, moaning on and on and on. See these pebbles here?"
"Er, yes."
"That, my friend, is you in a few months time; a bald, smooth pebble, who knows nothing better than to rest here gently until some large watery fish, or sea beast, decides to use you as mouthwash. So shut yer hole, you miserable, moaning, groaning, good-for-nothing bit of gravel."
"Right, well, I demand..."

The turtle moved closer and stared at the rock with great presence and severity.

"You are demanding nothing. You are no one and no one cares about you. You are the same as me, that limpet, that seaweed, those molluscs and those shallow water, finless wonders. So shut your trap, now."

"I'm not standing for this...!"

The turtle butted his beak up to the stony face.

"If you do not desist from your disgruntled ramblings, I will personally eat a load of plankton and then poo all over you. Then you will be a pointless, plankton-pooed, pebble. You won't feel any better, but you will be a lot stinkier. So shut it, you prize plonker."

"Well, I've never been spoken to like that before! This is outrageous!"

The turtle waddled away clearing his throat, as the limpets began to laugh.

"You come back here! I say, come back here!! You ruffian! You ignoramus! You come back and apologize! This instant."

The stone simmered down. It looked about at the life around it; the seaweed, the various mollusks, crabs, fish, other sea-life and the many smooth surfaces on the pebbles. It noticed how the once rugged edges of life had now smoothed, letting the seemingly soft waters shape the stones into pebbles.

"You get used to it," said the grey pebble. "You let it just wash over you in the end. No point in complaining. It might make you feel better, but when you give that anger to another thing, it don't want it, so it gives it to another thing, who then gives it to another thing, and so on and so on. Anger, you see, is the gift that just keeps giving, as no one ever wants it. That is until it is given to a pebble.

"And that's why we're so smooth, us pebbles. We just let it wash over us. The anger of others is subdued by us – nature needs something that can take that negativity, and that is us. You too will also become smooth like us, just you wait and see."

The stone sighed, looked about him and resigned himself to an aquatic life, at least for now.

It appeared to be quite quiet under the water, even tranquil and there was a serenity that began to permeate through to him.

That was until the turtle returned and sh*t all over him.

Shakya region, North India, 3rd July 590 BC,

about 3ish in the morning

A clatter could be heard, waking the resident of the room in surprise. The moonlight had moved away from the window, yet it was so bright, illuminating the palace walls and gardens.

"What are you doing? You'll wake everyone up!"

"I'm sorry, but time machines made out of tin aren't exactly devoid of noise."

"Well you should have made it out of wood, or something soft."

"How about I make the next one out of your brain..."

"Are you implying I'm soft in the head?"

"Sshh!"

"No, you bloomin' sshhh! Blithering idiot! You're going to wake the dead."

"Someone's coming."

"Who?"

"Someone."

"Quick, up here..."

"One mo' - mustn't forget the time machine."

The two cats jumped on to a wall then toddled along the thin edge towards a window then hopped on to the ledge before entering the room.

"Sshhh."

"Why are you telling me to shush? You're the one making the racket!"

"Sshh! Look, there he is. Apparently cats love to hang around his statues, all over the world."

"And snails."

"What?"

"And snails!"

"What have snails got to do with anything?"

Tinker tutted then looked at Marmalade with a look of almost complete contempt.

"Well, when he became Buddha, he also became bald and

one hot day snails saw him and didn't want him getting sunburn on his baldy head, so slithered up to his head to protect him. "

"You really are ridiculous, aren't you?" began Marmalade, shaking his head in disbelief. "Look... Are there snails here? Do you see any mollusk mop? No. Any gastropod garlands? I think not. Oh, maybe he's got extensions of worms weaved in to compliment his silken, snail tresses. You utter nincompoop! Look, he's got a full head of hair, see..."

The cats stared at the head of the adolescent child. Tinker moved closer. Then closer and closer still until he was close enough to touch him.

"What are you doing?"

"I wanted to see what he smells like."

"What?"

"I wanted to see..."

"No, no, I heard what you said, I'm just exclaiming 'what!' as in being surprised. And you can't see smells, unless you have synesthesia maybe..."

"He smells of peaches."

"Whoopee! I'm so happy for you! Now get here before... Too late."

The youth awoke suddenly after feeling the whiskers tickle his skin. Seeing the cats in the room took him by surprise. After rubbing his eyes, he sat up on his bed.

"And good morning to you too," he said as he petted Tinker.

Marmalade decided to get in on the cuddles and strokes and nudged his jaw along the boy's hands.

"Who might you be, eh?" asked the child metaphorically, then was completely surprised when Marmalade addressed him.

"I am Marmalade and this here is m'colleague, Tinker."

"Two talking cats! What a surprise!"
"That's not the best part, but we'll go with that... Are you Mr Gautama, Siddhartha – do you prefer Sidd or Esss for short?"
"Why, yes! Yes, I am. And Siddhartha will suffice."
"Good, well, as you're one of the most intelligent and enlightened humans in this world, I was wondering if you could help me."
"I shall certainly try, but I'm not so sure that I'm enlightened!"
"You will be, dude, you will be, trust us on this. Anyway, can you answer this: what has five letters, is not dissonant, musically, yet like a Mandarin or Cantonese – last letter is L?"

Siddhartha looked at them, bemused.
"What?"
"What has five letters, is not dissonant, musically, yet like a Mandarin or Cantonese – last letter is L?"

Siddhartha looked around the room in a puzzled way.
"I told you he wouldn't know," said Tinker.
"A load of chuffin' good you are then, aren't you! You may well find escape from suffering mate, but you're no good at crosswords are you? Come on, Tinker. Let us depart. Oh, and if you decide to shave yer hair off, watch out for the snails!"

Marmalade and Tinker jumped to the floor. Looking at their host, Marmalade bowed his head low as Tinker computed computations on the tin can, then they disappeared from sight.

Tilsit, East Prussia, 7th July 1807,

After breakfast

The small barge rocked on the agitated waters, reflecting the tension of the participants.
"Just sign the flippin' treaty already," demanded Napoleon. Nervously, the Russian Emperor signed the documents, leading Napoleon to shout to the staff on the bank.
"Now get me off of this stupid barge!"
The soldiers then pulled the barge towards the bank of the Neman River allowing the party to alight. Napoleon brushed the breath of the Russians off of his regalia then marched over to his caravan.
"Good. Now that the treaties are signed, I can celebrate. Tonight I shall have a personal celebration with my wife and tomorrow, to continue the celebratory spirit, I'd like us to hunt rabbits."
"Rabbits?" said Berthier. "But it is out of season in Russia."
"I want to hunt rabbits!"
"How about hunting some duck? That is more in season at the moment, even though strictly speaking, it's outside *all* traditional Russian hunting seasons."
"Rabbit, Berthier!"
"How about a petit canard?"
"I want rabbits!"
"Duck would be better..."
"Rabbit!"
"Why not duck?"
"Why not rabbit!?"
"But it's not hunting season!"
"Berthier, who is emperor?"
"You are, my imperial majesty."
"Uhuh! So I am declaring a rabbit season open. Alright?"
"But where shall I get rabbits from? There are none here."
"You are Chief of Staff, yes?"

"Oui."
"When we need more troops, you enlist and enroll more men, yes?"
"Oui."
"Then use those same skills to get rabbits!!! Do I have to tell vous how to do your job?"
Napoleon stormed off to his tent.
"Napoleon! Mon petit choufleur! Come here my darling," called Josephine from the privacy of the tent.
"Coming, mon radis magnifique."
Berthier shook his head in disbelief and racked his brain for a solution.
"How am I to 'enlist' rabbits when it is out of season?"
One of the Russian soldiers nearby happened to hear his dilemma. Cautiously, he approached the French Chief of Staff.
"Excuse me, Chef. I may be able to help you for I know people who breed rabbits. It may depend on the quantity required, but at least these people have, les lapins vous poursuivez, yes?"
"How many can they get for me?"
"How many do you want?"
"Well, we probably need about 3..."
"Three rabbits, no problem."
"No. More, so I will need 3..."
"30?"
"Non monsieur. Three...?"
"Three hundred?"
"Non monsieur, 3,000."
"You need 3000 rabbits? For a hunt? It wont be a hunt, but more of a rabbit party, or conférence pour lapins!"
And so Russian went away to acquire les lapins pour le Petit Caporal. It was quite a challenge, to acquire so many rabbits but the Russian managed to acquire a lot of them

via his contacts and other sources.

The next morning, many cages and boxes lined the far edge of a field, just outside of Tilsit, ready for the grand hunt. Napoleon's caravan and his entourage arrived and were greeted by his Chief of Staff, Berthier. The Russian soldier approached Berthier nervously.

"Have you got le lapins?"

"Yes, Chef, but I couldn't get the full 3,000."

"How many did you get then?"

"One thousand, eight hundred and fifty seven."

"Well, that will have to do. Right, let loose the rabbits and let's get the show on the go!"

Napoleon walked over towards Berthier with rifle in hand and a few hunting colleagues.

"Ah, Berthier! Are we ready for the big hunt? I'm looking forward to shooting some furry fiends."

"You don't like rabbits?"

"I can't stand them, with their constant twitching noses, those stupid long whiskers, lengthy ears and stupid buck teeth. They're a scourge, a pest, a needless and stupid animal. So I'm looking forward to killing some of them."

On the far side, the rabbits were released and gradually started to emerge from the boxes. Napoleon and his party began to move, hunting for rabbits. Slowly but surely, the rabbits emerged as the hunters progressed into the field. After a while, one of the hunters spotted a rabbit.

"Look, over there!"

One came in to sight, then another, then another and then more, then more still until at least 50 were visible.

"Why are they moving towards the party?" asked Berthier to the Russian.

"Well, it's not rabbit season and virtually impossible to find wild rabbits at the moment, so I had to find an alternative."

"What kind of alternative?"
"Domesticated rabbits."
"Domesticated? You mean pets?"
"Oui, chef."
"Hmm..."

As Napoleon gained ground with his colleagues, more rabbits appeared, and approached them.

"Good grief! So many! And more appearing," said Captain Fréman.
"Berthier, I thought you said it wasn't rabbit season?"
"It isn't your Imperial Majesty," said Berthier as he started to move away.
"So how come I can see a congregation of lapins approaching moi? Getting larger by the minute, the second!"
"I don't know."
"There's more, look," announced a very surprised Fréman.
"They're everywhere! Hundreds of them! Look!"

The mass of rabbits neared, getting closer and closer.

"How come there are so many?"
"If this is what it's like out of season, I'd like to see just how many there are in season! Look, there has to be at least a thousand rabbits! And yet more appear!"

The rabbits headed towards the hunters, getting closer and closer.

"Sacré Bleu! There's thousands of them and they're getting closer," said a nervous Napoleon.
"Shall we start shooting them?"
"We haven't enough rounds, maybe only enough for fifty rabbits. Where are they coming from..?"
"They're getting closer, mon general. What shall we do?"
"I don't know, but I don't like the look of them. Look at that one there, it looks evil!"
"They're moving in on us."

"I know! We're surrounded!"
"What shall we do, mon general?"

Napoleon looked about with fear on his face. The league of rabbits closed in on the hunting party, hopping forwards, eyes transfixed on the humans. The sea of fur edged slowly forward. Napoleon and his party started to retreat. With every hop forward, the hunters took a step back.

"There's nothing else for it; retreat. Run, run away. Run. RUN!"

"Mon general, quickly, this way!"

"Berthier. Berthier!! BERTHIER!!!"

The Chief of Staff was no longer nearby and had already made good his escape. Soon the Frenchmen's steps turned into a hurried walk, then into a run, then a sprint.

"Argh! Le lapin terrible! Dépêche, dépêche toi!"

As the running army retreated, the rabbits gathered momentum, causing the French to shout and panic.

"Dépêche toi, dépêche toi! Prendre la fuite!"

"Run!!!"

The Frenchmen made it to the caravan and hurriedly packed their things, all the while watching for the furry peril that gained ground.

"François! Mind le lapin! It's going to nibble your ankles!"

"I'm done for, your majesty. Leave me and go on."

"Summon the guard, the legion! Anatole, get the big guns, quickly!"

The rabbits were almost upon them, twitching their noses and hopping about happily. The cotton tailed menace approached the French as they left hurriedly. This was one battle Napoleon could not win, the battle of the rabbits.

"Maybe next time I will hunt ducks," he said, looking back at the field of rambling rabbits.

Egypt, 14th November 1152 BC,

Just after 2pm

"Take this down, Emi. Hand, comb, bird, backward arrow, wave, hand, eye, bird, squiggly thing..."

The court attendant came in to the throne room to address the Pharaoh.

"The slaves are revolting again."

"I know they're revolting, but can we be a bit more progressive, please?"

"No, Pharoah, they are actually revolting. Even the artisans are - they won't budge."

"I know they're revolting, especially with the lack of sanitation on the building site. Wherever you go you have to look where you're walking; if you're not stepping on a poor person, then it's minding one's step with all the faecal matter there."

"My lord, the workers are on strike – they are literally revolting."

"Oh, I see. Emi, be a love and pop back in a mo' would you. Oh and be a dear and send in my chief whipper, please."

"It's the new necropolis - they say it's back breaking and they aren't paid enough."

"Well, what is enough? It's somewhat subjective isn't it? And don't they know it's to *break artistic barriers* and usher in *innovation in architecture*? They're doing it for the love of art, aren't they?"

"No, they're doing it to get paid. And apparently not enough."

Suddenly, Pharaoh noticed two cats in his throne room. Marmalade approached, bowing low as he did.

"Tinker, turn on the translator thingy. O, Great, Magnificent Pharaoh type person, I am humbled that you entertain my presence. I believe this is my homeland, historically and that you venerate cats. However, my question is a simple one..."

The Pharaoh looked quizzically at the pussycat, probably wondering how it could talk.
"Oh, my! How wonderful, a talking cat has visited my kingdom! Praise the gods! Who sent you? Was it Bast?"
"No, we came via the medium of a time-travelling, tin can device, devised by m'colleague, Tinker."
"It was Bast, wasn't it! We've been blessed! Nefertiti, quickly, bring our guests some kibble!"
"That's nice, as we are a bit peckish, o Pharaoh. However, my quest is a simple one: do you know the answer to this; what has five letters, is not dissonant, musically, yet like a Mandarin or Cantonese – last letter is L?"
"I've no idea, love, but come, sit, let us inspect your long, golden hairs... And who is this?"
Pharaoh looked at Tinker, admiring the grey-black markings on him. Picking him up, he stroked his short hair.
"Oh, that's Tinker, whom I referred to earlier as m'colleague. He's a genius, but not very good with crossword puzzles, hence my quest. So, o great one, what has five letters: is not dissonant, musically, yet like a Mandarin or Cantonese – last letter is L?""
"I haven't a clue, my dear. What I do know Is that you've saved me from the end of year Bad-Luck demons."
"The what?"
"Bad luck demons. Anyway, you must stay."
Marmalade moved away over to Tinker who was fiddling with the tin can.
"Tinker, I think we're done here. They are hung up on outdated superstitions and can't solve my crossword problem.
"So dear Pharaoh, the time has come to depart. Thanks for the kibble. Tinker, hit it!"
The two cats appeared to flicker then disappeared from

sight, leaving the monarch in shock.
"They truly were magical moggies sent from Bast."

Somewhere, some town, no particular day,

Any time in the past or present

Mr Jaggers was an ordinary man, in an ordinary house, living an ordinary life, with an ordinary wife, along an ordinary road, in a nondescript town. He was in his early fifties and wore the same style of suit every day, had the same haircut since his early twenties and worked somewhere where no one really noticed him, in a business that wasn't essential, but necessary. For all intents and purposes, he was a boring person living a boring life. That was until one night when he heard the sound of glass breaking.

Someone was breaking in to his house.

His wife became disturbed and sought to shake her husband from his slumber, but he was already awake.

"Jaggers. Jaggers!"

"I am awake my wife. Hush now and I'll go and see what is happening down stairs."

So Mr Jaggers placed his slippers on his feet, put on his pajama top and placed his spectacles on the bridge of his nose. Quietly, he walked across the landing and trod gently down the stairs. Holding back a little from the living room door, he peered in through where it was just to, for he never closed the stairway door at night, save he might need to go downstairs for sundry things, like a glass of water, a rolled up newspaper to swat a spider or moth, or on the odd night when he had trouble sleeping he would descend for a nip of whisky, just so to settle his troubled mind.

His mind was very troubled, you see.

So Mr Jaggers looked through the door and saw a person dressed in dark clothes, looking through drawers, cupboards, sorting through papers and ornaments to assess the value of the things, so to take what they deemed worthy and necessary.

The thief was blissfully unaware of the host, unaware of Jaggers nearing him, oblivious of the object he had in his hand and never felt a thing when Jaggers struck him on the back of the neck. Calmly, he turned the thief on to his back. Then he proceeded to the shed, removed the roll of plastic sheeting, the shovel and utility knife. Then nonchalantly, he wrapped the body in the plastic, cut the roll where the covering sufficed, taped the plastic at the join and went to the garden. He began digging in the ground, making it just deep enough, then placed the body in the ground in a cavalier manner and resumed his shovelling activity by replacing the soil.

"Hush now, don't make a fuss."

Taking his slippers off at the back door, he placed them in the bin liner, took it out the bin and walked barefoot to a neighbour's dustbin and placed the bagged, soiled slippers within. Calmly walking homeward, he entered the house, ascended the stairs and got in to bed. He took off his pajama top and snuggled down to rest.

"I shall need some new slippers, my wife," said Jaggers.

"Oh, not another burglar again was it?"

"I'm afraid so, my wife."

You see, the burglar was so used to breaking in and stealing, just as Mr Jaggers was so used to killing people, for he had been a soldier, in the war. In everyday life, when people become so used to things that are wrong, there's no difference between that and what's right; it's just another ordinary day, in another ordinary town, for another ordinary man, who lives in an ordinary house, with an ordinary life. What would be most extraordinary, is someone saying, "That's wrong!"

Then we can start to make things right.

North-East England, Spring, 2016,

After Breakfast

"Right, that's it. I've had enough of this; I'm going on holiday! Michael keeps saying I should get away from it all and just 'chill,' so I will."

With that statement, God began walking out, followed by a concerned angelic secretary.

"But where will you go?"

"I'm telling no-one, but I am taking this mobile thingy with me, so you may contact me should there be an emergency. And I stress, only an emergency. I'm sure Michael & Gabriel can look after any impending issues. I shall be *incognito ergo sum*."

The secretary's face dropped and for a moment she was lost for words. Following God hurriedly, she began to stutter, "W, well, you know what happened last time don't you? All that Lucifer business? Sh, surely you, d-don't want that to happen again?"

"Look, Jemima; that is your name isn't it?"

"Yes..."

"Jemima, do you know how long it has been since I had a rest?"

"Er, 8 days ago?"

"Now don't start that whole '8 days' thingy! Do you know how difficult it is to change the cosmological constant?"

"No, I, I meant it was 8 days ago; Raphael looked after the heavens whilst you had a wander around the garden."

"Was it that recent? Seems like an eternity. Well, anyway, I'm going on holiday. Nos vamos!"

Somewhere on planet Earth is a particular beach that God likes, where unique circumstances caused the pools to be rust red and glass pebbles to be scattered over black sand. A tall, solitary fragment of a cliff stands like a sentinel in the middle of it, looking out over the sea. God walked down the large, rugged steps set in the bordering cliff face, deckchair under arm, found a pleasing spot then sat down. Seagulls barked overhead, wild birds twittered, the long wild grasses from up on top of the cliff path could be heard rustling in the breeze, which also soothed the warm brow.

Unless you knew this was God, you would not know, for God looks just the same as anyone else and here God sat, on the favoured beach, peacefully. Taking out a book and pen, God began annotating, A Brief History of Time, by Prof. Stephen Hawking. Now, not many people know this, but when God does happen to go on vacation, the occasional cigar is enjoyed, as is a drop on a certain Chardonnay. So there God was, sipping wine and relishing a cigar, annotating A Brief History of Time, the sun was warm and friendly, the beach was quiet and the sounds around and about were at one in the moment. Then the mobile phone rang.

"Hello? Hello! Hello? Hellooh? Sorry, sorry wrong button... Marjorie, so good to speak to you... Er, well.... Not at the moment... Can we reschedule? I'm sure it can wait... It can't. So you are telling me that time and tide wait for no one? Do you know who you are talking to? No, I'm not being ficitious! All I am saying is that I'm sure deciding on what colour the icing should be on Ghandi's Heavenday cake can wait until I'm back in the office. Where am I? Out, dear, out, that is where I am. Thanks, thankyou, thankyou... Yes. Absolutely.... Love to. Bye, bye, bye!"

Taking a gentle, long draw on the cigar, God sat back in the deckchair and sipped some wine. The annotating began once more.

"Einstein-Rosen bridges my eye!"

The pen crossed out a swathe of writing. In its place the words, 'toast rack' were written. This was then crossed

out and ‘cosmic springs,’ took its place.
“Should confuse the String theorists!”

Smoke gently lifted into the air as a Herring Gull swooped overhead. The wine was nearly supped and once more, God relaxed. Then the phone rang again.
“Hello... Hello.... Hellooooh? Hello, sorry wrong button. Hi, Marie. What? What... What... What do you mean? But that’s impossible! Have you... Have you... Yes. Have you... I don’t wish to appear rude, but please shut up, just for an eon. Have you used anything recently? Er, washing machine, tumble dryer, kettle, er, toaster... Ah, right, well, go to the downstairs cloakroom, look at the fuseboard... (Fuseboard?) I mean the consumer unit. Yes, yes, now flip the switch... No, flip it. Flip it. I said flip it, dear! Never mind, I’ll send Nikola over. Y’know, the nice young man, went a bit paranoid and bonkers... No, not er, not.... That’s right, not Philip K Dick; Nikola, Mr Tesla, dear. I’ll tell him to pop over. Alright, all...okay. Okay, love to, but can’t. Okay, bye... Yes, bye... Bye, bye!

“Can invent the x-ray machine but can’t flip a simple switch.”

Placing the phone back in its pocket, God stretched out then reclined under the noon sun. Heaving a sigh of relief, God reached for the glass, grasped it lightly and lifted it, spilling what little was left over the book, for the phone had rung, again.
“What is it!? What is... Hello, helloooh? Hello! HELLO! Sorry, sorry, wrong button. Yes, G here, who’s this? How did you get this number? It’s ex-directory. No, no I’m really not interested. I don’t need life insurance, thank you. Goodbye.”

The phone was once more placed back where it belonged. God took a deep breath, then another, and another, leant back and relaxed. The spoiled book lay on the dark sand, wine bleaching the pages and the cigar was nearing its end. Gently, God nodded off to sleep. Then a buzzing could be heard. Stirring, God looked around but could see nothing flying nearby, then deduced it was indeed the mobile, yet again.

"Hello, hello? Ah, hang on, got it. Sorry wrong button. Jemima, how can I help? Is it urgent?"

"Well, yes and no really. It's the atheists, they're causing a scene in the Cafe Costa Fortuna."

"Jemima, the atheists are always causing a fuss. If this is what happens when pardons are given, I shall have to have a rethink."

"Apparently there's coffee everywhere and Buddha's tried to ease their suffering, but they're just not listening. They just keep going on about how they want an espresso machine in the lounge! They state that they need a wider range of coffee, rather than the ones offered in the cafe."

"Is Siddhartha with you?"

"Yes, one moment..."

"Hello?" asked Buddha.

"Now, Sid, my dear chap. Do me a favour, tell them all that this is it, I won't put up with it any longer. If they want an espresso machine, they need to clean their act up and stop creating such a fuss."

"It all seems to be about having some, er, some sort of afterlife crisis."

"What's that supposed to mean?"

"They say that they didn't know you existed until they died and this has negated their existential angst. They feel that more evidence should have been given them in order to make a decision of faith. They weren't expecting eternity, they feel it was thrust upon them without choice."

"Well you tell them they're being ungrateful. Negating

existential angst, my eye! What more evidence did they need? Were recycled atoms and stardust not enough evidence for them? Tish and tosh! Get them told! If they want an espresso machine in the lounge, they need to stop this silliness. And if that cafe is not all cleaned up by the time I come back, there will be no espresso machine, no cafe, and no 7th heaven privileges!"

"Well, I'll tell them, but they are very upset you know."

"Get them told! And if they don't do it, tell Moses to turn all their straws into ducks, so they can't drink milkshakes either!"

"Okay, okay, will do. Namaste."

"Yes, you too, er... have a nice day. Sorry, Namaste.'

A groan of frustration was emitted as God went to rest again on the deckchair.

"Negating existential angst... Tut."

Another book was plucked, as if out from mid air, and God was reading through, The Book of the Book, by Idries Shah.

"Is that it? That was short! Ah... Ah, very clever, very clever. Nice. Yes, nice twist at the end."

At a flick of the wrist, the book transformed into a novel by Will Self. At yet another flick of the wrist, it morphed into, The Trial, by Franz Kafka.

"Will Self! Not reading that nonsense! A bit of Kafka, I think... Therefore, I am. Will Self... It can't be his real name!"

As God read the story, it began to form an idea of how the atheists could be handled, but at once God decided against it. Thumbing through the pages, peace descended upon the beach.

A seagull pooped on God from above.

"Now, really, there's no need... Really... There is plenty of shoreline y'know!"

Wiping the poo away with one hand, the other placed the book down. As the poo disappeared, the blessed phone rang yet again.

"Hello? Hello? (Green button, green button). Hi, sorry, wrong button. Hello?"

It was Jemima. "I'm ever so sorry to disturb you again, but it's just that there's a little bit of a problem."

"What sort of problem?"

"Well, y'know how that nice young lass, Leanne, is asking for good weather so the cyclone won't hit the coast of Tonga? Well, it means we'll have to adjourn the tsunami that wipes out the coast of California. The two things are going to be an issue. We can't do one and allow the other to go ahead..."

"Uhmm... Well, we can postpone California I suppose."

"The other thing is, Mr Fujimoto is asking for good weather for the wedding of his daughter when rain is due for the same day, for the farmers of Okinawa, so they can have a better crop yield..."

"Tell you what, drop the cyclone, make it a hurricane. Regarding the Japanese.... Light, occasional showers for Mr Fujimoto and a good downpour at night for the farmers. Just downgrade it all basically."

"Right. Oh and just one more thing; Mr Lewis has been fighting with Mr Tolkien. Apparently, Mr Tolkien says that Middle Earth is far better than Narnia. They've been going at it hammer and tongs!"

"Tell them that both are equally as nice. I can't decide between the two. Explain that its like deciding between Star Wars and Star Trek."

Taking a stroll, whilst humming the Star Wars theme music, God decided to head for the nearby seaside town, for hunger was creeping up quickly. Venturing along the coastal footpath, God could see people walking their dogs. Some were gracious enough to wish, 'good day,' whereas others were more interested in their own company. A harbour breached its way into the sea, welcoming various ships and bidding, 'Bon voyage' to others. The sea lapped up at the shore and all seemed well. In the distance, God saw the ice cream parlour, which decided what food to eat. Walking a little further, God ventured in to the parlour and spied the menu. Several people were in line for the counter, so God waited, patiently. Six customers later, God decided on which flavour to have, Fudge-Choc'Chip.

"Good afternoon, could I have two scoops of Fudge-Choc'Chip, please?"

"I'm sorry, we're fresh out of that. We've got..."

"Ah, right. Well, I'll have, er, Choc'n'Roll please."

"Er, sorry. Out of that one too, I'm afraid.," said the young woman, in a thick Mackem accent. "Sorry."

"Okay then, I'll have the... How about... Ah! Cherry Blush."

"One moment... Sorry have none left I'm afraid."

"Don't be afraid, for I Am with you. Errrr...... Chunky Funky Donkey?"

"No, sorry."

"Caramel Marshmallow?"

"No..."

"Strawb'n'Dairy?"

"Er.... No, sorry."

"Do you in fact have any ice cream here?"

"Yes, we've got...."

"No, don't tell me, I want to guess. How about Rockin' Raspberry?"

"No."

"Minty Munch?"

"... No."

"Choo-choo Chewing Gum?"

"Er, no."
"Fudge'n'Fruit?"
"No..."
"Blueberry Blanc?"
"No, sorry."
"Er, Banana-nana Meltdown?"
"Ah... Sorry, no."
"How about vanilla?"
"We don't do vanilla."
"Don't do vanilla?' It's the great British favorite! How can you not do vanilla?"
"Not much call for it around here! That'll surprise you. But we do have..."
"No, I'm keen to guess; Toffee Coffee Hemorrhage?"
"No. Sorry."
"Er, Gannin' Yem Jam? What on earth is Gannin' Yem Jam?"
"It's clotted cream with strawberry jam, covered in toasted breadcrumbs, with a hint of hyssop."
"Hyssop? Don't see that in recipes much these days. Have you any?"
"Let's see.... Er, no."
God sighed. "Katie Custard?"
"No."
"A Mere Trifle?"
"No."
"Zesty Link Bucket?"
"No. Fresh out of it."
"Couscous Truffle Mousse?"
"No."
"Gannin' Mad For It?"
"Sorry, no."
"Mint Mad Hatter?"
"I'll have a look.... Sorry, no."

"Monkey Blood'n'Guts? (Sounds revolting)?"
"Er, no."
"Do you actually have any ice cream? You state that you have over 99 flavours. Do I have to go through all of them?"
"No, I'm sorry. We do have a little of the Almond Apple Avalanche, but actually we're closed now. I was deliberately wasting your time until we closed."
"Heavens above! You mean that after all that you're now closed?"
"Aye. Sorry."

Exiting the parlor, God gave a frustrated sigh and mumbled something about forgiveness, whilst walking away to the nearest takeaway. Having ordered a large mixed kebab, God began walking along the seafront, back towards the beach. Evening was setting in, the sun was moving steadily towards the horizon, leaving ripples of red, orange and yellow dappled across the sky. A purple hue came through as the birds began to find their way home. Suddenly, an electronic version of Vivaldi's Autumn burst into life. Throwing the kebab accurately towards some pigeons and seagulls, God answered the phone.
"Here we go again! Hello, hello? Heh... One moment! Sorry, wrong button. Yes?"
"Hi, God?"
"Speaking."
"Hi there, it's Janice from marketing. Do you have a moment?"
"Go on..."

A strong American accent was emitted from the ear piece, badly muffled by having the phone too close to her mouth. "It's about the new campaign? We were wondering if you would be able to change something in the Pater Noster? Well, it's where people say 'daily bread,' we were wondering if you would mind changing it to a nonspecific brand, as the company, Daily Bread, are considering legal action due to it being an infringement on their copyright and trademark."

"Oh, good grief! You are joking?"

"No, I'm being very serious. We have a letter here from Dewey, Cheatem & Howe, their lawyers, asking if we will change it."

"Eurgh! Oh alright, change it to... To regular serving of bread. Is that okay?"

"That should resolve the issue. Oh, and whilst I have you, do you remember our discussion about the perception management campaign? Well, we have some ideas around how we could put across a new image. We're considering a photoshoot where you're using a selfie stick to take a picture of you and a group of marginalised individuals, of various ethnicities, representing inclusion. Angelina Jolie and Richard Gere are very keen on that idea...?"

"Good grief, no! I'm not appearing in any photoshoot, for anyone, until the end of the world happens. Even then it'll only be a brief visit. Speak to Mary, maybe she will be interested; she likes making special appearances. Word has it that she's popping through to make an appearance at Lourdes again soon. Is that okay?"

"I suppose so. Anyway, sorry to have troubled you. Bye."

Janice parted company and left God to ponder what would happen if this was a permanent vacation? How would everyone cope? Who would they turn to? The thought of so many unanswered prayers made God feel sad. There was faith, but mankind had still not fully embraced this miraculous gift, so they could resolve their own issues. As this thought lingered, the phone rang once more. This time it was an automated message.

"Have you been mis-sold PPI? If so press..."
"The hang up button? That reminds me, must speak to Edison about how we can stop automated dialling..."

No sooner had the phone been put away, it rang again.
"What is it!? What, who? Oh! Wait, wait.. Sorry, wrong button! Hello? Who's this? Can't I have moment of peace?
"Ah, Mr Chopra! I've been meaning to have a word with you! About this mumbo jumbo you come out with... What did I say? Keep it simple!! Occam's Razor, my lad, Occam's Razor. No, I'm not asking you to change your brand of razor! Deepak, have you never heard of Occam's Razor? Keep it simple. The message is too contrived; you use way too much ineffectual language. Just explain how to live, simply, effectively and peacefully. It's not brain surgery!

"Right. How is Oprah? Good, good. Well, it was bound to happen... No, no. Not at all, bye, yeah, bye... Haha, very good. Yeah, bye, bye... Bye.

"How do you work the answer thingy on here?"

Whilst God fiddled around with the phone to activate the voicemail, the walk to the beach continued.

Upon opening the email application, God noticed 10,563 unread messages and this had only been in the space off a few earth hours.
"Oh, who did a group message? Steve Jobs... Oh botheration! Someone's done a 'reply to all!' Really gets on my nerves..."

Someone was organizing a surprise party for Ghandi, to celebrate the anniversary of his entry into heaven, so consequently everyone was emailing details to each other to make arrangements. One email was addressed to God directly asking if the celebration could be held in the refectory. Agreeing that is was a great idea, a reply was sent with haste. There was also the usual junk mail; meet

local-single women in your area, you have won money in our prize draw, and how to reduce body fat and become body-beautiful in just 7 days. One email bought God's eye, from Mr Vinicius Gotanga, who lived in Nigeria. By some fortunate happenstance, he had come in to a considerable amount of money and wanted God to put it into a bank account, until such a time when his late uncle's estate is resolved. This raised a cheerful chuckle as God read the mail. Did people really think this sort of thing was real? Spending a moment in thought, a willing of protection over less witting individuals was sent.
The email box was now clear, reports were 'mark all as read' and the deckchair was finally in sight.

As the night sky was coming out to play, God looked at the stars and remembered each one. An occasional shooting star passed in the sky, as the sea became calm and drank the lush, full moon.

"There you are! I remember when you were just a twinkling in my mind's eye, yes you. And you. Oh, those were the days... Where's that little nebula? Aha, there you are! Beautiful. Oh, you're all beautiful. Such splendour, such diversity. This makes it all worthwhile, a moment like this, looking up at my garden. You are all very special you know! And you..."

A little spider crawled on God's hand and moved quickly over the palm, then forefinger. Placing the spider down gently, God reclined under the diamond filled sky. After a short while, rest turned to sleep, as the waves soothed the busy mind of God.

A vibration was felt. It repeatedly resonated, making God aware of an incoming call. Stirring from sleep, God answered.

"Hello? Hello? Ah, wait a moment, (why do I always press the wrong button? Every time...) Hello?"

"Hi, it's Jess, from Advertising."
"How can I help?"
"We've had an enquiry from a car company, wondering if we'd be interested in making a deal to promote their new model."
"Uhm. Go on..."
"Firstly, they're asking what car do you drive?"
"I don't need a car, dear; I move in mysterious ways."
"Yes, but if you were to drive one, what would it be?"
"Oh, good grief, that's a tricky one. Er, probably a Fiat."
"Oookaaay? Why's that?"
"The prayer, my dear, in fact it's my prayer, 'Fiat voluntas tua, sicut in cælo et in terra."
"Ah, right! Got you. So could we change it? From Fiat to maybe... Mercedes?"
"Er, not sure."

God ran through it under his breath, "Mercedes voluntas tua... sicut in caelo... Mercy will be done in heaven, let it be done... Uhm, it's possible..."
"Well?"
"I prefer Fiat really... It says it better. Plus, I think the legal team would be none too happy with the changes."
"So that's a no to Mercedes then?"
"Yes."
"What? Yes, that's a yes, or yes that's a no?"
"Yes, that's a no."
"Okay. It was worth asking. Bye for now."

Dawn roused the birds and the sun opened the flowers, whilst reflecting off of the sea. Checking through the email inbox on the phone, God scanned over the subjects quickly to discern if there was anything of importance. There was one from a Buddhist, that had no attachments, even though it displayed a paperclip icon; there was also was a curious email from the auditors regarding the regular audit of accounts, for apparently, it wasn't enough just to credit righteousness to each account and 'forgive us our debts,' wasn't necessarily a good enough reason for them. With the amount of write-offs God sanctioned, this had to comply with the statement, 'each of us shall give an account of himself.' Making note of the date the auditors were due in the calendar, God flicked through the remaining messages.

The only trouble with becoming temporarily corporeal, to have a holiday, was that even though God remained omniscient, omnipotent & omnipresent, God liked to experience the realm as other humans do, hence the mobile telephone. Also hence the interruptions. God did begin to ponder over how mankind had ever managed to live without the mobile devices for so long and remembered the simplicity of life before electricity and radio. There was enjoyment through waiting for a postcard to arrive and time to read a book without being interrupted. As God mused over this, the phone sprang to life and the ringtone for the 'crisis of faith hotline' (Help! by the Beatles) was emitted.

'Hello, hello? Ah, green button.. Hello? Ah, Rene, you again. What's up this time?"

"Well, I'm concerned about the statement, 'I think, therefore I am.' Does this mean when I'm not thinking, I am not?"

"Look, we've been through this before. You are still being, even if you think you're not thinking. By simply thinking that you're not thinking, you are in deed still thinking."

"But how? If I really am not thinking then I can't be being! Can I? Subsequently, I am worried that I don't exist!"

"The very thought of thinking you're not thinking means you are thinking! You can't negate your existence by not thinking!"

"That's what I thought."
"Therefore, you are! See?"
"I think so..."
"Have you been talking to Schrödinger again? Him and that annoying cat?"
"Maybe..."
"You have, haven't you! How many times have I told you, stay away from him. He likes teasing you and thinks you are gullible."
"I'm not that gullible! Anyway, merci beaucoup, best go; Pavlov's ringing the bell for breakfast."
God ended the call and dialled a number straight away.
"Hi, G here. I'm looking for Thomas, Thomas Merton. Okay, I'll hold.

"Ah, Thomas! Just the fellow. Do me a favour please, as I Am is on holiday. Would you and Suzuki send some Zen monks to nip round and see Descartes please? Yeah, it's the whole thinking without thinking thing again. Schrödinger set him off. Brilliant, that's brilliant. Thanks ever so much. Bye!"

God walked up from the beach and went searching for some fruit. Soon enough, a raspberry bush revealed itself and God picked some, then ate them whilst moving along the path. Venus could still be seen in the early morning sky and whisps of clouds hesitated over the land, waiting for the wind to decide which way to go. It was nice, just to enjoy nature and creation. God wandered along, talking to the plants, greeting beetles and wishing a good morning to the starlings. Above the nearby field, a hawk hovered, looking for food. Gracefully, it dived then swooped up to fly away. Taking the stroll meant going through the neighbouring fields of a local farm and God did so, being enraptured by the colours and crops.
"And who might you be?"

A voice shouted at God, but discerning where it came from was difficult. "Oi! What d'ya think you're doing?"
"I'm just taking in the morning air."

A farmer waltzed over to where God was. "Get off my land! All the same, you tourists, trampling my crops! Get away!"

God was concerned about the use of the term, 'my,' that the farmer used.
"Whose land is it?"
"Mine!"
"I'm not causing any harm! Surely the land is free for anyone to walk on?"
"Nope! This is my land!"
"And how did you come by it?"
"Was my great grandfather's and he handed it down to my father, who handed it to me."
"My dear boy, you merely lease it. The land is a gift to everyone. You don't own it per se."
"Oh, I see. You're one of those clever ones, aren't you? Go to university to earn a degree then think you're all high and mighty!"
"(You're sort of right on the high and mighty, nevertheless...) So you are prejudiced as well as particular!"
"Get off my land, gan on! Away with you!"
"Alright, alright, I'll go. Wouldn't want to upset you now would I?"

God moved off of the field, muttering things to one's self. The farmer watched, making sure that God was off of his land.
"Maybe I should smite him; haven't done any smiting in a long time. Nothing like a good smite. No, no, I mustn't! That's naughty. I smite thee... No, no, no... Curious word isn't it? I smite, he was smote, she was smitten – hang on,

that can't be right?"

Moving along the roadside, God journeyed to the small retail park, where an assortment of shops, cafes and businesses were. A wild cat followed behind, miaowing gently. God petted the creature then set it on its way. Descending down the hill to the shops, traffic began to make noise and civilization made its mark known.

Going into a clothes shop, God viewed the rails of garments. People jostled about as if they might miss out on an opportunity for a bargain. This was too busy, so God went to another shop, which sold gadgets. It was amazing to see the ingenuity of humankind, just as much as it was interesting to see the clutter they wished to own. The amount of unnecessary devices in the shop reached a level of ridiculousness. Who would want a door handle handler? Why not use the handle itself? The product bore the inscription, 'Ideal for those with phobias!' There was a device which enabled you to find your keys, with another device to help you find the device, which helps you find the keys. Pointless. There was a backscratcher with inclusive shoehorn; brilliant for midgets who want to scratch their back, whilst putting shoes on; a soup-spife, a soup spoon that's also a knife; emergency soap dispenser – ace for cleaning your hands in an emergency; a pen that doubles as a nose-picker; a whitehead squeezer, with complimentary blackhead squeezer; a portable toe cushion; a rechargeable recharger that recharges rechargers; an emergency coat hanger, that can also be used as a set of tongs; a bracelet made from fool's gold that keeps idiots away; an infinity timer, with a battery life of 2 years; a cable that allows you to connect your phone to a toilet paper holder, so it will not fall down the loo; an open mesh cage to keep flies in; grow your own laundromat; a miniature hedge trimmer for bonsai trees; dissolvable water tablets – just add water; insect cleaner; do-it-yourself autobiography kit, pen not included; miniature microwave for peanuts; dust deterrent, not to be used in confined spaces; emergency inflatable hygienic hair trimmer; build your own conservatory, bricks not included; dissolvable door knocker, not for external use; design your own tattoos, imagination required; occasional carpet cleaner, for any occasion; Quantum-tom Sat-Nag, gives directions to destinations whilst travelling at light speed, batteries not included; replacement light bulb for cat's eyes; colour blind spectacles for traffic lights, 'go when it's not red!'; Higgs-Boson detector for vacuum cleaners; How to read a book, a handbook for first time readers; a ladder for frogs; self-filling bird feeder, seeds not supplied; self-fulfilling deluxe prophecy kit, will power required; a 3 part course on how to overcome procrastination, parts 2 & 3 not included; and many, many more useless items were on the shelves.

Memories of the great flood came to mind and God wondered if it was time for another one. Casting aside the idea, God went to have a drink. The cafe was large and quite full. Taking place in the queue, God looked at the beverages on offer.

"Hi there, what can I get you?"

"I'll have a regular, Chocochino Mocha please!"

"What size?"

"Er, regular, like I just said. Sorry if it was confusing."

"Can I have a name for the coffee?"

"Er, Chocochino Mocha? Or is that too obvious?"

"No, like a name, so we can write it on the cup, so we know it's yours."

"I therefore name this cup, Donald."

Once the coffee was ready, God sat at a table for two

beside the window, so to watch the people passing by. The world seemed so full of busy people doing pointless tasks, like statistics for statisticians, with only the few doing meaningful work. God watched the public meander along the precinct; mothers with children, dragged them along to shops under protest and couples, early in courtship, held hands that induced vomiting from friends. Men in smart suits also walked hurriedly with a phone surgically attached to their ear. All passed by, unaware that God was watching out of the cafe window, sipping at a hot, chocolatey coffee. God thought about the modern world and how it had changed, then sighed.

"Well, that's what happens when you dish out freewill," came out, not realising it had been vocalised. Then the sound of Vivaldi broke train of thought, for the phone rang.

"Hello? Hello? Heh.. Ah, hang on... Green button... Hi? Who's this?"

"My name's Jeremy. I heard that you had a road-traffic accident in the last five years."

"Did I?"

"Er, yes. Did you pursue a personal injury claim at that time?"

"Goodbye."

A little blue light began to flash on the mobile phone. After some detective work, God worked out that there were notifications on the Facebook profile. God had been opposed to the idea of having a Facebook account, but had been talked in to it by Janice, Gabriel, et al. Loading up the application, there were 32 friend requests, including one from Richard Dawkins and another from Simon Cowell. Suggested friends still had the grinning face of a undertaker playing an accordion, of which God had no idea how they knew each other. God has also been tagged in a post, along with 16 others, by David Icke, so consequently all comments that were subsequently posted, God received notifications of. Flicking through the posts on the wall, God saw various gifs of fluffy kittens falling off of things, adverts for dating sights, videos that 'you really must see – this had me lol-ing for hours!' Or 'I actually cried with laughter at this...'

"No you didn't, you lying little...," was God's audible criticism. Why did people think it was so important to share their lives on social media? It frequently made God wonder about it. Why should anyone want to know about Richard Branson having his first poo in a commercial spacecraft, or how Kim Kardashian achieved a perfect pout by injecting botulism into her lips? The only thing worse than this was the hash-tag syndrome that was the latest fad: #whyareyouallidiots?
#isleptwithsomeoneshocker
#epic_fail_shocker_pigscantfly
#imnotacelebritybutimightbepossiblybypostingthis. And what was with the need to promote seeming nobodies to celebrity status? God was bemused by this. What about the everyday heroes no one knew anything about? 'Woman saves child from drowning,' was surely a better headline than, 'Snorkeling idiot discovers he can breathe underwater!'

After the silent rant, the phone rang. This time the green button was pressed without hesitation.

"Hi, God?"

"Speaking."

"Jemima here. We were wondering when you'd be coming back. It's just that there's a meet and greet scheduled for this afternoon and St Peter says he's sick to the teeth of doing them."

"Can't you ask someone else to do it? How about

Zoroaster?"
"I asked him already, but he said he was busy contemplating eternity."
"Oh well, I suppose I better get back then."
"Thanks and sorry."
"Don't worry. See you in a bit."

God switched the phone off then manifested into the heavenly dimension. Entering the office, God saw a mountain of paperwork on the desk and several people waiting to gain attention. Michael, the archangel, smiled and approached.

"Have a nice break did we?"
"Not too bad. If I go away again though, I am not taking the mobile phone!"

And with that, God got back to work.

Castle in State of Chu, May 12th 248 BC,

Teatime

A wanderer sauntered up the dusty track to the castle, being watched all the while by the two gate guards. The nearer he got, the more the guards gathered their wits about them, trying to guess who he might be. Finally, a knock on the gate brought one guard down from the guard-post down to the gate.

"Who goes there?"

"Evil warlord's messenger."

"Who?"

"I'm a messenger of an evil warlord."

"You're a philosophy salesman."

"No, messenger from an evil warlord."

"You're a philosophy salesman."

"No I'm here to bring a message to King Zhuangxiang, personally."

"You're a philosophy salesman and not a messenger sent from an evil warlord."

"Yes I am."

"Whose the evil warlord?"

"Eh?"

"Who sent you?"

"Er, Wei... Wei Chunshen."

"Really?"

"Yes, Wei Chunshen."

"Interesting name... And what's the message?"

"Ah, well that's only meant for the King."

"Hmm. Well, I shall let you in, but if you are a philosophy salesman, he will chop your head off. They are always coming around here, trying to flog their ideals and values. Xiong Yuan will execute you if you're a salesman..."

The secure gate was opened allowing entry to the alleged messenger, who smiled and began his entrance to

the stronghold.
"Have you considered the benefits of Mohism though and its contrary position to Confucianism? How we should have universal love for everyone and not just filial loyalty? Or have you considered the stance of Wu Hsin in relation to progressive Daoism?"
"Right, off with his head! Take him, Xiao."

Thus the other guard took him away to have his head chopped off.
"Have you considered wei wu wei, maybe, and the benefits of traditional Daoism along with ancestor worship? Great combination there; keeps the families happy and great talking point at dinner parties."
"Shut up."

The salesman continued to talk as Xiao tried covering his mouth. Resisting, he struggled to get away but was unsuccessful, so Xiao began to hit him.
"Oh, I see, trying to suppress the teachings are we? Have you thought about the ideology of Zhuangzi and how ethical relativism is relatively ethical? Eh?"
"Sooner we chop your head off the better."
"Are you displaying the violence inherent within your system? How about a more peaceful approach like Chan Buddhism? Do you like sitting whilst looking at walls? Great for loss of ego."
"Bloomin' philosophy salesmen!! Shut up!!!"
"You can't suppress the Dao and express violence! The Dao existential school meet tomorrow; you should come along, make some friends and explore reality."
"Will you shut up!"
"On Tuesday's we examine objective reality, juxtaposed by Zhuangzi's argument that reality is purely subjective according to one's environment. Have you heard the parable of the Mantis?"

"The one where he loses his head?"
"Yes. Ah, so you're aware of this work."
There was a pause, then the thud of the axe as it removed the salesman's head, yet the head still spoke.
"How does this fit in with your views on epistemological scepticism? Eh?."
"You're dead, so shut up."
"Ah, but you only think I'm dead due to the axe chopping off my head, when actually, I'm not dead, because I believe I'm alive."
Xiao shook his head as he thought about it.
"If you believe you're alive and I believe that you are dead, where do we go from here?"
"Well, that my friend, is a very good question. Tell you what, we'll call it quits if you can chuck my head over to those flowers, so I can take in their aroma."
So the guard tossed the head over to the flowers.
"I don't believe this!" said Xiao.
"Well, if you use my approach, you'll always be a-head."

ISC Spaceship, Tau Ceti III, stardate: 23.1.2349,

Around 1930hrs.

"Three is good, two - good and one is good. Em status - positive. Thrusters are at low and boosters are fully charged."
"Confirmed. That's affirmative, Capt. Innes. Systems are online and all good."

The starship, Tau Ceti III, moved gently and silently through space towards the outer rim of the Rnadnorri solar system. It had a modest crew of three; Innes, Hauser and Kashoggi. Their current mission was to return to the planet Terra Prima and establish communication with the galactic neighbours. The inhabitants were humanoid and spoke in a language similar to ancient Sumerian and this journey was to be one of many where relationships could be established with them.

The crew of three was just big enough to stop the insanity stemming from loneliness and bring their many talents into a unity, whereby they weren't merely astronauts and scientists but also ambassadors and diplomats. Each had their specialist areas, but together they were harmonious in navigating the ship to its destination.

"Kashoggi, I'm picking up an anomalous reading. It says that there's 2 more people on board."
"It must be a malfunction. Run a diagnostic and then reboot."
"I have and it's stating there's 5 onboard. It's altered the carbon dioxide state and oxygen levels have dipped slightly."
"Well, there's no one else on board!"
"I know."

The crew set about trying to discover the cause of the anomaly, searching high and low.
"Have you checked the sub-conduit ducts?"

"I'll check now," said Hauser and made his way through the series of narrow passages. Nothing unusual was spotted and the mystery deepened. The Nacell tubes were spotless, the compartments clear and air locks secure. It was if two small beings, maybe ghosts, were on board.

"Innes, come in," called Kashoggi. "Have you searched the food storage?"

"Negative, but I'll check now."

Going to the food storage compartments, Innes, heard a noise, a like a liitle hum.

"Kashoggi, check carbon dioxide levels in FS#Alpha."

"There's a slight increase in there. FS#Kappa has a more noticeable increase."

Moving cautiously, Innes neared the food compartment. The hum became louder. Peering around the corner, he saw two small beings, eating food, with empty foil packets cast aside.

"I would say, 'Good morning' or 'Good evening,' but my biological clock is rather out of sync at the moment."

"Who is that?" asked Kashoggi, over hearing the conversation on the communicator.

"Tell your man that we're friendly, if you will, please. My name is Marmalade and this here is m'colleague, Tinker."

"How'd you get in here?"

"Never mind all that. Assure your crew that we are friendly, please. Hmm, the tuna casserole is rather nice!"

Innes announced through the intercom that the two beings were cats, talking cats at that, who were not a threat.

"What are they doing?"

"Eating!"

"Yes," started Marmalade. "We were traversing space-time and became a little peckish, so we popped on board

for a snack. Hope you don't mind."
"Er, no, I suppose not."
"Good. The liver and onions isn't up to much, but the pepperoni, penne and sun-dried tomato sauce is absolutely top notch!"
"How did you get on here? In here? How?"
Tinker tossed aside a foil container and looked up at the captain.
"We've discovered how to use quantum tunneling, compensating for Heisenberg's uncertainty principle of course, to travel through space and time, and consequently land here on your ship, Tau Ceti III."
"How did you manage to get these exact co-ordinates?"
"A simple variable; on a journey not greater than your current trajectory and no less than where you travelled from, your location varies according to your speed, which isn't known, so according to all the possible points and various speeds of which you could have used, the probability of us landing on a craft is relatively simple when the route is known. It's the translocation of molecules that is the real problem, so the vibration of our molecular structure alters as to that of of your ship, thus enabling material objects to translocate relatively easily and move through dense materials and space. As for time, a suspension of the internal body clock is necessary, so the temporal-molecular sickness, commonly experienced by travelers, such as ourselves, is overcome. So combining these simple ideas allows us, along with this tin can, to traverse space and time, to land on your ship."
"Er, okay... I think."
"Anyway," Marmalade interjected, "We have more pressing concerns. I have a question for you; what has five letters: is not dissonant, musically, yet like a Mandarin or Cantonese – last letter is an L?"

"Eh?"
"What has five letters: is not dissonant, musically, yet like a Mandarin or Cantonese – last letter is an L?"
"Er..."
Marmalade rolled his eyes.
"Look, you're an intelligent person - a qualified lawyer, scientist, diplomat and Olympic gymnast - so I figured that you would have some idea of a relatively simple crossword conundrum such as this, but all I'm getting is an 'Err' and 'Eh.' Do you make sounds resembling any other vowels, or is that beyond your capacity?"
"Errr..."
"Good grief! And this, Tinker, is the captain! Let's see if anyone else has any sensible ideas."
The cats wandered off, leaving Innes bemused and behind. Strutting in to the cabin, Tinker spotted Hauser and nudged Marmalade in his direction.
"Excuse me. Hello. Now, I wonder if you'd be a dear and pour us a bowl of water please."
A stunned Hauser agreed and set about getting the cats a bowl of water.
"How did..."
"Look, we've been through all that and the author hates having us repeat ourselves, so bally well buck up with the water please. Thank you. Now, tell me, what has five letters: is not dissonant, musically, yet like a Mandarin or Cantonese – last letter is an L?"
"I'm sorry, I'm just struggling to take this all in. You're cats, capable of talking and travelling through space-time, yet have landed on our spaceship to ask a question?"
"Yes, I'm somewhat vexed, I can tell you! So we've been searching for the answer by meeting people who we deemed intelligent enough and capable of answering such a question, but still it eludes us! And some of them aren't

that bright, I can tell you! No. Christopher Columbus? Absolute idiot with no sense of direction who merrily bumps into lands unknown willy-nilly as a fortunate happenstance! Then there's Galileo; the great nincompoop he is; it was me who suggested to him that the planets orbit the sun, as he thought they were orbiting some mysterious gravitational body near Venus!"

"What about Schrödinger, eh," said Tinker.

"That buffoon? Says we exist in two states simultaneously and tried to get me in that blinkin' stupid box to prove a point! I think not!No, I don't think so. And then there's that ultimate ignoramous, Oscar Wilde. 'We're all in the gutter looking up at the stars,' are we? No, no we're not! Some of us have made it to the stars, per ardua ad astra mate! Absolute numpty!"

"So what is it you want exactly?" said Hauser, trying to get them back to the topic at hand.

"An answer."

"To what?"

"Good grief! I'm surprised that you're not still in diapers being spoon fed morsels of ignorance by the dozen! The question, my good man, is what has five letters: is not dissonant, musically, yet like a Mandarin or Cantonese – last letter is an L?"

Hauser paused and thought. The other crew members had joined him by now on the deck, listening to the conversation.

"Hello? Anyone in there?"

"Er..."

"For pity's sake! Is there no one in this universe that knows the chuffin' answer? All I'm getting is 'Umm,' and 'Err.' And they let you lot travel to a neighbouring solar system to build a relationship with Earth? They might as well sent Donald Trump! Come, Tinker, let us go posthaste and find more intelligent life."

And with that, the cats disappeared from sight.

"Houston, we *had* a problem," announced Kashoggi.

"Receiving you, Ceti. Go ahead."

"We've encountered alien life, I think."

"Not the Banana Ablution Society again is it?"

"No, it's time travelling cats who can talk."

"Yeah... We know about them."

"How?"

"You do not want to know. Suffice to say that the NSA, CIA and other agencies are aware and still researching it."

"Where have they come from?"

"We don't know, but our best staff are looking into it."

"What have they found so far?"

"Not a lot. And we still don't know what has five letters: is not dissonant, musically, yet like a Mandarin or Cantonese – last letter is an L."

Pottsville, Virginia, 18th May 2071,

Around 2pm

The landscape was a combination of arable farmland, beautiful countryside and farmsteads. Fields were littered all over with horses and cows. The rough track, that was assumed to be a road, led the cats due east and consequently they were exploring their current environment. The patchwork quality of the fields brought different hues of yellows, browns and greens to prominence under the somewhat grey skies that loomed. The sun crested the furthest clouds, like gold gilt cotton wool.

"I hope it doesn't start raining, as there's no one to groom me if I get wet."

"I'm just wondering why we're here at all," said Tinker as he checked the tin can once more. "Yep, it's definitely 2071."

"What on earth is going to happen then? I wonder if we can get any info from this cow."

Marmalade wandered over to the field and looked up at the cow who peered over the wire fencing.

"Hey, moode! I'm terribly sorry to disturb you, but I was wondering what on earth actually happens around here as it's frightfully boring."

"What's a moode?"

"What?"

"What's a moode?"

"Sorry, let me explain; I'm a male cat, so I'm a dude, female cats are dudettes; you're a cow, so you're a moode. So, moode, what goes on around here? What's the gossip?"

"Nothing, it's sure boring around here."

"But this is 2071 and something important should have happened, or be happening."

"Nope. Nothing going on here."

Marmalade looked away is dismay.

"Tell me; if a cow can't produce milk, are they an udder failure? Or are they just a milk dud? Hahahaha."
"Ha,ha, yeah really funny, like I've not heard that one before..."
"Oh, come on, moode, lighten up. Things aren't that bad. At least you're not steak yet, or a beef-burger, or sausages."

The sun peeked out from one of the clouds suddenly, illuminating the corn field nearby and revealing how the breeze moved like a wave through the sheaves, or a corn tide moving to the hilly shore.
"Is nothing going on around here? This is boring, Tinks. It's totally boring dude."
"It doesn't seem right," said Tinker.

The clouds suddenly peeled back and a huge silver ball shaped vehicle descended, making a strange noise, like a hazard warning signal. Three mechanical legs then emerged at the base of the sphere and it landed on the ground next to the cow field. Some silver-blue lights flashed as they travelled around the circumference of the craft's waist. A loud, piercing sound then announced the opening of a circular door on the underside of the sphere.

Then carefully and cautiously, two beings emerged. They were very small balls of white fluff each with huge, wide dark eyes, a tiny round mouth,appearing to have no legs but two long feet, each having two long toes and very long arms with hands that had small palms and three long, chubby fingers. Looking almost cute, they noticed the cows and the cats and moved towards them. Standing approximately a meter away from them, they both stopped and said, "Ooooo! Teenie pushkit!"

Their voices were very high pitched and they looked amazed at the cats, not the large cows in the fields.

"Teenie pushkit! No-ee gerblinsk. A ta-tah teenie pushkit! Ooooooo!"

Marmalade and Tinker looked at each other.

"Hello. My name is Marmalade. This is Tinker, m'colleague. Who are you? Or what are you?"

"Ooo! Teenie pushkit tak, in tak jae, jae gubbit."

"Tah bay, teenie pushkit!!! Inter ver-gnarlycot! Teenie, teenie pushkit!"

"Er, yes. Me Marmalade, this Tinker. Who are you? Do you understand?"

The balls of fluff talked between them in a hushed manner. Marmalade nattered with Tinker, asking why the translator wasn't working, to which he explained that it only worked with known languages and phonics – the alien language and dialect was obviously nothing like anything it had heard or been calibrated to previously.

"Teenie pushkit!!! Awwwwww, teh-teh-teh-teh-teh-teh-teh-teh-teh-teh-teh-teh. Varmeh pushkit ver-gnarlycot."

One of the fluff-balls began stroking Marmalade and making the repetitive noise, whilst inspecting him closely.

"Okay, okay: I think we are the pushkits, Tinker. I'll try another tactic...

"Us, we are teenie pushkit, yes?"

"Teh. Teenie pushkit ver-ger-ger-gnarlycot."

"Yes. Me teenie pushkit. You? What are you? Who are you?"

"Ter-hahahahahahahaha! Verbner cajoulie melonkoff . Da ta geese."

"What? They seem to understand me, so why can't I understand them?"

"Verbner cajoulieeeee melonkoff, serceeteee da ta geesheeee."

"I'm sorry, I don't quite understand?"

"Da ta serceeteee geesheeee."

"I think they want you to guess," said Tinker.
"Tehteteteteteh."
"You want me to guess your name?
"Tehtehtehtehtehteh."
"Er, okay."
"It'll help me calibrate the universal translator to their language as well," explained Tinker.
"Right then: are you Martians?"
"Nahanahnahnahnah."
"Are you Saturnians?"
"Nahnahnahnahnah."
Are you from our solar system?"
"Nahnahnah."
"Are you from our galaxy?"
"Nah."
"Are you from very far away?"
"Tehtehtehteh"
"What is your planet called?"
"Verbner cajoulieeeee melonkoff, serceeteee da ta geesheeee. Da ta serceeteee geesheeee."
"You want me to guess? With all the possible words, combinations of words, sounds and intonations, you want me to guess?"
"Tehtehtehtehtehteh."
"Here goes then, Tinker. There's nothing else but to go for it: I am going to have to deduce their name by trying every conceivable combination of sounds and words.

"Are you Aay?"

"Nah."
"Are you Beee?"
"Nahnahnah."
"Are you Cee?"
"Nahnahnahnahnah."

"Are you........"

1 hour later

"Are you the Shed? The shed people?"
"Nahahnahnah."
"Are you the, er, tin?"
"Nanahnahnanah."
"Are you the Fleas?"
"Nahnahnahnahnah."
"Are you Skips?"
"Nahnahnahnah."
"Are you the, er, the Spots?"
"Nananahnah."
"Are you - *oh, this is taking forever* - are you the Kevin?"
"Nahnahnahnah."
"Are you the James?"
"Nahanahnananana."
"Are you the Kit?"
"Nanananananahnah."

8 hours later

"Are you hair?"
"Nahanahahahahana."
"Are you lint?"
"Nanananananahnahnah."
"Are you specs?"
"Nahanahahahahana."
"Are you day staff?"
"Nah."
"Are you the other job part time traffic lights partake in thereof?"

".... nahnahnahnah."
"Are you beetles?"
"Naaaaaahnahanahahahahanah."
"Are you a type of stick?"
"Nahnahanahnahnahnahnahnahnahnah."
"Are you weevils?"
"Nanahnahnahnahnahnananananahnah."
"Are you Toilets? Toilet people?"
"NAHNAHNAHNAHNAH."
"Oh, strong feelings there. Are you wood chips? Are you chippies?"
"Nananananaannaahnah."
"Are you nitwits?"
"Nanananananahnahnahnahna."
"Are you pretty?"
"Nanananananananahnahnahnahnahna."
"Are you grains?"
"Nananahnahnahnahnanaana."
"Are you trying to drive me potty?"

4 hrs later

"Are you the Puts?"
"Nah."
"Are you the puglets?"
"Nananananananaanah."
"ARE YOU THE Tinglyspingly?"
"Nanananah."
"Are you the - *I think I've tried every word and sound in the human language*- are you the Pigswill?"
"Nahnahnahnahna."
"Are you the upswaylee?"

"Nahnanananananananah."
"Are you the wigglenbogensie?"
"Nahnooonoonahnahnah."
"Are you the Leicestershire County Rowing Comittee?"
"Nahahnahnah."
"Are you the supoywangiylilyweh?"
"Nah."
"Are you the spoons? Spoon people, are you spoon people?"
"Nanananananahnahnahnah"

3.5 hours later

"Are you the strawberry farfalle?"
"Nanananana."
"Are you insane?"
"Nah."
"Are you the vanilla fudge cake sandwich?"
"Nanananana."
"Are you the only beings in the universe without a freakin' name?"
"Nananananananaanah."
"ARE YOU the Fitzwilliam Bandwidth?"
"Nananananananaanah."
"Are you the Navajo needlework network?"
"Nananananananaanah."
"The piebald luncheon meat pie crust?"
"Nanananana."
"The teriyaki tango troupe?"
"Nanananananaa."
"Are you the placebo chicken company?"
"Nannanah"
"Are you the, much maligned, potted potatoes of Pisa?"

"Nanananananananaanah."
"Are you the slightly left of center conservative coconuts?"
"Nah."
"Are you the savoury tidbits, miraculously left over from a Oprah Winfrey buffet?"
"Nanananananananaanah."
"Are you the leftovers from grandma's New Year's Eve party?"
"Nananananananananahnahnah."
"Are you trying to make me mentally unstable?"
"Nanananananahnahnahnah."
"Are you the aloof barbers of Beirut?"
"Nah."

2 hours later

"Are you the random, yet collective, memories of Salvador Torres?"
"Nahnahnah."
"Are you the noodle jogging sounds of suburban high life?"
"Nahnahnahnah."
"Are you the sons of Derry custard bagels?"
"Nanananananananaanah."
"*Oh, will it never end...* Are you the wonky crumpet stuffers of Camden market?"
"Nananananananahnahnahnah."
"Are you the, oh, are you the collective mindset of Minsk gerbils?"
"Nahanahnahnahnahnanana."
"Are you the unsurrendered whims of incontinence, wrought by eternal angst?"

"Nah."
"Oh help me! Tinker, I can't go on much longer. Are you the Saboteur Sextuplets of Stevenage?"
"Nanananananaan."
"Are you the nihilistic badgers, anti-shaving brush campaign lobby?"
"Nanananananaanah."
"Are you the top percentile of investigative Shintoists who love to hate hamsters?"
"Nhanahananah."
"Are you vegetarian, insurance salesmen who love falafel?"
"Nahnahnahnahnahnah."
"The detuned carrot section of the New Hampshire Philharmonic Orchestra?"
"Nanananananana."
"Are you - *I'm losing all hope now* - Are you the top 100 fans of Weird Al Yankovic?"
"Nah."
"Are you the sons and daughters of a being called Ned?"
"Nanananananana."
"Are you the Kilimanjaro ethics committee?"
"Nahanahahahahana."
"Are you the deranged construct of a surreal and curious mind?"
"Er-tehtehteh-Nananananananaanah."
"Oh, you had to think about that one, didn't you. Are you the, the, are you the Banana Ablution Society?"
"Tehtehteh."

There was a pause.

"Are you serious!?"

"Tehtehtehtehreh."
"The Banana Ablution Society? Tinker, we've got it! They are the Banana Ablution Society!"
"Tehtehtehteh."
"By jove! It only took 17 and a half hours to discover our aliens are the Banana Ablution Society! I'm so happy..."

Marmalade started crying hysterically.

"Who'd have guessed; the Banana Ablution Society! *How obvious*! Why didn't I think of it earlier? This is amazing, but, I am inclined to ask, why?"

The aliens gestured to the pussycats, guiding them on to the spaceship and through a series of snapshots on the large screen, they saw the Banana Ablution Society taking selfies at various locations within the universe, whilst dealing with bananas.

"And how does one clean a banana?" enquired Marmalade.

One of the alien creatures waddled over to a compartment and took out a banana, then proceeded to cleanse it.

"Oh no! Tinker, don't look!. That's revolting, eurgh, oh... oh, oh, I see... Ahhh! Oh, that's really quite clever!"

The Banana Ablution Society continued wittering on whilst showing the photographs and pictures on the vast screen. There were many scenes of bananas in various galactic regions and planets capable of sustaining the propagation of bananas. At one point, the alien, who was for all intents and purposes the leader, showed pictures of their home planet and solar system. Apparently they come from a planet called, Jim, which has mountains that look like they are made from semolina. This lay within the Cheed sector of the Vraah galaxy, somewhere near the outer rim of Noputtyfrim.

After several more pictures of their home world, Marmalade became more curious as to why they were in the back of nowhere, some county, USA.

“Why the deuces are you in Pottsville? There are no bananas here.”

After a lengthy explanation, and pointing at various components of their ship, it was discerned that there was a problem with the quantum-tom-tum, sat-nav thingy.

“Thankfully, Tinker here, is a wiz with stuff like that. Let him have a look at it.”

And so Tinker began tinkering about with the craft, with lots of Banana Ablution Society members coming to meet the ‘teenie pushkits’ and stroke them, much to the annoyance of Marmalade. If this didn’t annoy him enough, he was also subjected to having every member of the Banana Ablution Society onboard take selfie photograph with him.

Ideas Dept. at CIA HQ, Virginia, 25th October 1965,

Teatime

"Maybe if we integrated some equipment in to a parrot and augment it so that it's able to send us sound and pictures? Do you think that would work?"

"I'm not sure. Parrots can talk, so they might start repeating stuff we have said."

The agents were trying to figure out new ways of gaining intelligence in a covert manner. The current project was gaining some success and critical acclaim, prompting them to keep the ball of positivity rolling.

"The only thing is, how many parrots are native to Russia?"

"That, my friend, is a very good question," said Agent Timmins.

A sudden flash broke their train of thought as Marmalade and Tinker arrived in the office.

"We discovered aliens, dude," announced Marmalade, rather excitedly. "They're real and fluffy and ever so cute, and they got this weird way of eating, and they've got this really weird purpose in life, and they take lots of selfies, I mean a lot of selfies."

Timmins was very taken aback with the wash of information.

"It's true," said Tinker. "They glow this weird colour when they're excited and love bananas, and they are really advanced but have a very peculiar language."

"Whoa, whoa there! You've actually discovered alien life? This isn't the greys again is it, everyone knows that was just propaganda and invented to appease the masses."

"No, these aren't the greys, they are called, the Banana Ablution Society."

The agents looked at each other, Timmins raising his eyebrows.

"Okay, let's get this straight, there are aliens called the Banana Ablution Society."
"Yes," said Marmalade. "They come from the Cheed sector of the Vraah galaxy, somewhere near the outer rim of Noputtyfrim, on a planet called, Jim, where there are mountains made from semolina."
"How do you know this?"
"They took us there, dude. They took us there."
"And what do they look like?"
"They're cute, little fluffy things, no taller than Tinker and they've got ever such short legs, long feet, short arms and hands with only three, long fingers. They have these huge, big puppy eyes, no nose and when they think or meditate, they glow purple and when they're excited they glow yellow."
Timmins laughed at the cats.
"How do you know that they are called, the, the, (what was it)... The Banana Ablution Society?"
"Believe me, I know. After *seventeen* extremely long hours, we discerned this was indeed their name."
"And these aliens, what do they do?"
"Their sole purpose in life is to traverse the universe, cleaning bananas wherever they find them. It's kinda weird, I know, but, but it's what they do."
"And how exactly do they clean these bananas?"
"You do not want to know, dude! Believe me, you don't want to know. If you knew, you'd probably never eat a banana ever again; no banana mañana or ever, no!"
"This all seems a little odd, if you ask me. Where's the proof?"

Tinker opened the tin slightly, to take out two photographs and took them over to Timmins. The pictures were of selfies, taken by the Banana Ablution Society, which included the cats at differing locations, one of which had the semolina-like mountains in the background.

"They are absolutely obsessed with taking bloomin' selfies, dude. This one is of us on Jim, their homeworld; there's me looking kind of cool, can you see and look here, you can see Happenie, he's the pilot & Sturverm, his colleague. See, they're so small and cute and fluffy."

"Their planet is called, Jim?"

"Yeah, dude, it's Jim. Shall I say it Tinks, eh? Shall I do the joke?"

"Go on, you're going to anyway at some point," said Tinker, looking in despair. "He's been laughing at his own joke all the way back here..."

"So, dude, these aliens, they live on the planet Jim, yeah? Well, that means, there's life ***on*** Jim, but, hahaha, there's hahahaha, huhuhahahaha..."

"Just tell them the freakin' joke!"

"It means that there's life ***on*** Jim, but not as we know it! Ahahahahaha-hahahahahahaha!"

Marmalade fell about in fits of laughter. The agents didn't know why it was so funny. Tinker raised his eyebrows and explained that there's a popular television program called, Star Trek, and the joke was a poor take on an expression the science officer, Spock, used. However, due to the time travel, Marmalade had failed to realize that his joke wouldn't be appreciated, until the series premiered in 1966.

"Marmalade. Marmalade, they don't get it, as Star Trek hasn't aired yet, that's next year."

Marmalade continued his hysterical laughter and repeating, "There's life ***on*** Jim, but not as we know it," much to his own amusement. The agents looked at the photographs with interest.

"How long did it take you to get back here?"

"Too long," answered Tinker staring at his partner in time, who was still laughing. "They are a highly evolved species who developed an Em drive, which has no propulsion, strangely. It uses some sort of magnetism which affects the quanta, thus the negatively tuned strings vibrate at a frequency different to the sub-space frequency, which pulls them through space, as opposed to pushing. It's amazing really. They've knowledge of how to trans-locate themselves seamlessly within space-time, by altering the frequency of their DNA. With them, it's all about sound and vibration. Basically, by altering the resonance of the DNA, they can transport themselves over vast distances, regardless of the cosmological constant. Utterly fascinating..."

"Yet their sole purpose is to clean all the bananas in the universe?"

"Yeah – turns out that bananas are the only fruit/herb that can be grown outside of our atmosphere and are abundant in M-class planets across the universe. It's something to do with how it's the seed of a herb."

"Hmm," said the other agent in the room, making note of the discoveries. "Have you brought any of them back with you? As we'd like to study them further."

"Yeah, about that. We figured you'd just dissect the little guys, so we didn't bring any here. And unless you have a spaceship with an Em drive, you won't be colonising their planet either. So, it's just these pictures and the knowledge that we aren't alone in this universe."

"So, Banana cleaning aliens, eh?"

Tinker smiled then called to Marmalade and as he joined him, Tinker operated the time-machine and they disappeared.

Kaminogō, Japan, Spring 1562,

Around midday

"What in the freaking name of sanity is going on here? Mind that sword! That looks bloomin' sharp! Tinker, lookout!"

Swords, spears and other sharp implements clattered above them. To the rear of them was a castle, from which more soldiers came screaming in to battle.

"Tinker, I think we better move, dude."

Marmalade and his sidekick moved out of the way rather hurriedly, as samurai rushed forward in attack. Some ninja and other samurai moved towards others opposing them, engaging in battle.

"Hello? I was wondering if you could help me at all? Hello, you. Yes, you with the pointy mask on; where are we exactly? Is this Norwich? It might explain the masks...'

"Anata wa koko de nani o shite iru no?" came the reply from the samurai who passed by.

"Tinker, the translator thingy isn't working, dude! Be a dear and fix the bloomin' thing."

Tinker began tinkering with the tin can and then the device on his collar. Another warrior ran past. It stopped when he saw the golden haired, Persian puss and tabby, greyed grimalkin.

"Why fish cat great finding and seize good!"

Marmalade looked confused.

"What language is this, Tinker? I don't understand him," he said, then addressed the samurai oncemore. "Hello. I'm sorry, I don't speak gibberish. Er, take me to your leader."

"Great cat fish siege good for us."

"I am a cat, called Mar-ma-lade. He is, Tin-ker. We speak to your lea-der?"

"Great cat fish siege. Good."

"Think, I've fixed it," proclaimed Tinker as he slapped Marmalade around the neck. "Try now..."

"I no Catfish. Me cat and you idiot. Me no speaky idiot. Take us to see your leader, o great thing..."
"You great sign and omen for this siege. We will take you to our leader."
"About bloomin' time!"

The samurai picked up the two cats and took them to the daimyo. The lord sat on a short stool, watching the battle. He smiled widely as he saw the cats approach. After stroking his moustache, he nodded and beckoned them near.

"Hmm. We have been blessed by a visit from these cats! It means our siege and attack does bode well. Greetings to you."

After being placed on a lacquered table, Marmalade nudged forward and nodded toward the daimyo, respectfully.

"And greetings to you, great person whom I don't know how to address. We bring you grand tidings and a bounty of blessings. In return you must answer me a question. "
"What do you ask?"
"O great thing, your siege shall go well if thou can answer me this: what has five letters: is not dissonant, musically, yet like a Mandarin or Cantonese – last letter is an L?"
"What?"
"What has five letters: is not dissonant, musically, yet like a Mandarin or Cantonese – last letter is an L? O magnificent person."
"I haven't a clue, I am sorry."
"Well, you're a load of no good then, aren't you!? Tinker, hit it!"

Then, in an instant, the two felines vanished, leaving the daimyo feeling a little odd. He blinked his eyes, shook his head then stroked his moustache and laughed a sudden, single chuckle.

On the way to Gettysburg in Pennsylvania,
19th November 1863, Around 9.30-ish

“I just don’t know what to write,” said Lincoln, scratching his head as he sat on the train.

Putting pen to paper once more, he started scribbling. *Conceived in liberty, delivered in the labor of equality, we face a war of which the fallen lay not a stone throw from here, having given their lives that we may live. They may slumber, but not in vain.*

“No, no, it doesn’t feel right.”

Abraham looked out of the carriage window, musing and seeking inspiration. Somewhere within aural perception, he heard a scratching sound and looked for where it came from. Seeking its location, he looked about and saw two cats trying to gain his attention.

"Well, as I live and breathe! How did you two get in here?"

"Good morning, Mr Lincoln! My name is Marmalade and this here is m'colleague, Tinker."

"A cat that talks! My, my!"

"Yes, I know. I'll skip the conversation where we ascertain how i can converse with you, if you don't mind. Getting to the point, I need your assistance. You're a wise and clever man and I'm wondering if you can assist in answering a question of mine."

"A question, eh? Well, I'll attempt to help you if you can help me. "

"Whatever, dude."

"I'm giving an address this afternoon and struggling with what to say."

"Never mind all that. Tell me; what has five letters: is not dissonant, musically, yet like a Mandarin or Cantonese – last letter is an L?"

Lincoln was surprised by the question and contorted his visage, as if in deep thought.

"Please, repeat the question."

"What has five letters: is not dissonant, musically, yet like a Mandarin or Cantonese – last letter is an L?"
Abe's face pulled the same expression once more as he thought long and hard.
"I'm afraid that I have not a clue."
"Well, you're no chuffin' help are you!"
"Now, for you to fulfill your part of the agreement, I need help with my oration for later this very day."
"Well, how about starting with a joke? That always breaks the ice and puts people at ease. How about something like... What do you call a dog with no legs? You can call him whatever you want, he's still not coming. Hahahaha. Or, if you're American when you go in the bathroom and American when you come out, what are you in the bathroom? European! Hahahehe. Get it, your-a-peein'! Hahahaha. Oh, I like that one. Or maybe, why can't a nose be 12 inches long? Because then it'd be a foot!"
"No, I can't use a joke..."
"Not even the European one - that's one of my favourites."
"No, I'm dedicating a cemetery, so it would be wholly inappropriate."
"Uhm, no, it wouldn't go down very well then. What have you written so far?"
Abe handed Marmalade the paper for him to look at. It was thick with scratches on that imitated writing.
"My word! You've awful handwriting, dude. Anyway... *Conceived in liberty, delivered in the labor of equality, we face a war of which the fallen lay not a stone throw from here, having given their lives that we may live*. Uhm, not bad, but try something like... 87 years ago, some dudes got together and traveled, to what is now, our great nation. Here we found freedom and that's being tested by this civil war."

"Not bad," said Lincoln, snatching the paper back and scribbling some notes down. "Eighty seven years ago..."
"How about making it sound more poetic? Like, 'Four score and seven years ago'?"
"I like that! It sounds even better. Four score and seven years ago, our fathers brought forth on this continent a new nation..."
"Finding freedom..."
"No - conceived in, in..."
"Liberty?"
"Good, good! Liberty and dedicated to the notion..."
"Or, to the proposition?"
"Yes! Dedicated to the proposition that all men are born equally. "
"Try this; dedicated to the proposition that all men are *created equal*."
"Brilliant! Thank you, Marmalade. Now we are engaged in a great civil war, testing whether that nation or any nation so conceived and so dedicated, can long endure."
Marmalade moved back and nudged Tinker.
"Writes a good speech doesn't he!? But doesn't know 'what has five letters: is not dissonant, musically, yet like a Mandarin or Cantonese – last letter is an L,' does he!"
And with that, the cats disappeared from sight as Tinker activated the tin-can time machine.

Nazareth, September 23rd 7 AD,

Just before Breakfast

"Joseph! That table is still wonky. You're supposed to be a carpenter, so fix it."
"I know, I know. It wasn't me that made it."
"Well, fix it!"
"I will Mary! Give me a chance..."

It was early in the morning when the cats arrived at an, as yet unknown, location. It was sandy with ad-hoc spots where wild grass grew. It appeared to be a hamlet with a small-holding, as a donkey, a few sheep and two goats lingered around.
"Where are we dude?"
"Somewhere in 7 AD... One moment. Looks like we are in Nazareth," replied Tinker.
"The band or the place?"
"The place."
They wandered around looking at the surroundings, taking in the sounds and smells. Three huts housed three families and the small-holding had a sort of workshop with a large hut, a stable and a cave within the nearby hillside.
"More precisely, we have arrived on September 23rd, 7 AD in Nazareth," confirmed Tinker.
"Good morning, donkey dear. I am Marmalade and this is m'colleague, Tinker. Any chance of finding some fish or kibble, please, as we're a bit peckish after our travels."
"I'm an ass."
"Oh, don't be so down on yourself!"
"No, I am an actual ass. Not a donkey. And you can find some food over there by that workshop."
"Thank you ever so much. This way, Tinks."

"Joseph. Joseph! Where's my cloth? You haven't been wiping sawdust with it again, have you?"
"No, I haven't. It's right there in front of you."
"Where?"
"There!"
"Well why didn't you say so!"
"I did. You just don't listen."
"I do blinkin' listen! Unlike you. That table is still wonky and the stable needs cleaning out."
"I know! Stop going on about it."
"Well, I wouldn't have to go on if you did as I asked. Jesus, get in the bath or you won't get your birthday present."
"I am in the bath."
"No, you're hovering over it! Get in and wash! Especially behind your ears."

The cats watched from a distance as Mary asserted authority about the home. The goat wandered over and showed some interest in the activities.
"Jesus!"
"I know. Tinker that's Jesus, dude."
"That's actually him... and it's his birthday?"
"Doesn't surprise me. Humans tend to make things fit as they want. It's not so much a history as it is a version of events."
"But that means that Christmas should be in September!"
"Yeah, I know. So it weren't in the bleak mid winter, coz it wasnt bloomn' bleak and it certainly weren't chuffin' winter. It was in early autumn. That'll upset the carolers! They'll have to rewrite all the Christmas songs and carols, save, O come, O come, Emanuel, and O little town of Bethlehem, and anything that starts with 'O-.' SoTinker, this means that we must write a song for Jesus birthday."

So the cats went away to rewrite a suitable carol for Jesus's birthday.

"Happy Birthday, son," said Joseph, as he handed Jesus a large, wooden box. Opening it, his face lit up as he lifted out his present.

"Thanks, Dad. Thanks, Mum."

James with his other brothers and sisters came in to the hut to celebrate the birthday.

"Enjoy your 9th birthday," said the children as they began tucking into the food that lay on the big table.

Later that day, the young Jesus went outside to do some chores with his brothers and sisters. As he walked the dusty land, he heard a strange noise.

"Pssst. Pssst! Pssstt!!! Over here..."

The cats were calling him over to a lean-to that housed a trough with feed in.

"Hello, Jesus, us humble catlets have come here to celebrate your birthday. As a preamble, I'd just like to apologize for how we got things so very badly wrong in the future, after you, er , you er; well we won't go into that. Anyway, back where we come from people sing carols on your alleged birthday and we would like to sing one for you. We have re-written it just for you though. So here is our humble gift to you. It's to the tune of 'In the Bleak Mid-winter,' suitably re-written for the circumstances of your humble birth. Tinker: A 1,2,3..."

The cats started singing.

"At the start of autumn,
No frosty winds did moan
Earth weren't hard as iron
And water certainly weren't like stone.

"Leaves were falling, leaves on leaves
And sannnnd blew on sannnnd
No, it weren't in the bleak midwinter
Long, long ago."

Jesus smiled and clapped.
"Jesus, have you fed those donkeys yet? And what's that awful caterwauling?"
"I'm just doing it, Mum. Thank you, that was a lovely song, really lovely and I very much appreciate it."
"So glad you liked it and.. Jesus, take care of yourself dude. You're a nice lad and you're going to turn out alright. Just take care."
"I will," said Jesus as he turned to walk on. "Oh, and Marmalade, take care dude. Tinker, you too. Shalom."
Jesus continued in his chores as the cats seemed starstruck.
"Tinker, he called me, dude! Jesus called me, dude!!"
"Yeah, yeah. C'mon on, let's get going. We've got to fix this mistake about Christmas," said Tinker as he computed the space-time co-ordinates to go back to their own time

Tuesday, 29th March 202, 72 Tewkesbury Avenue,

Before Supper

A young dog ran about happily wagging his tail. Finding a chewy, rubber bone toy, it picked it up with its mouth and ran around Marmalade. It was a small canine, that looked like it had a mixed heritage, probably of Maltese and Jack Russell breeds, and its colouring was of dusty browns and auburn. Its dark eyes were bright and playful and overall it seemed like a very happy dog. It dropped the toy then started licking Marmalade.

"Get off of me," Marmalade protested, but the small dog persisted with licking.

"Come here, let me help you regurgitate your food!"

"Stop licking me, you ignoramous!"

The dog stopped and sat in front of him, smiling its head off, wagging his tail frantically, eyes wide and bright.

"Hello!"

"Your licking has already sufficed in welcoming me."

The effervescent puppy wagged his tail.

"You're lovely, you are."

"That's nice, but you don't really know me yet and I fear your feelings may diminish somewhat when you're more educated about my good self. I wish to know if your feline fellow is here."

"Mildred?"

"Yes, Mildred."

"She is, but I don't know where exactly. Keeps hiding when I'm nearby."

"Hmm. I wonder why," said Marmalade in a rhetorical manner. "Mildred, o Mildred! Come hither please."

No cat emerged, but the puppy began running about again.

"This is my favourite toy. It's a bone and it squeaks! See."

The squeaking started in earnest, causing Marmalade to raise his eyebrows.

"Yes, very nice. Mildred! Come and save me from this idiot."

"I'm not coming out," said a voice. "He'll only lick me all over."

"Mildred, come out this instant!"

"No."

Marmalade looked at the dog.

"Look here, dog, do you promise not to lick Mildred when she comes out from hiding?"

It wagged its tail.

"Er... Yeah."

"Your long pause before the affirmation leads me to believe otherwise. You will desist from licking the cat when it comes out, do you hear me?"

".... Okay."

"Now listen, dog. Mildred will come out and you will not lick her, okay?"

"..... Right."

"Your tail is still wagging. Stop it. Mildred comes out and you no lick-ee - Right?"

The dog wagged its tail, looking very playful. Marmalade wasn't sure the dog understood or comprehended the instructions.

"Listen to me: Mildred no like-ee the lick-ee. When pussycat comes out, leave her alone. Do you understand?"

"Yeah."

Marmalade still wasn't sure the dog understood, but called for Mildred once more. Cautiously, the timid tabby emerged from behind the sofa.

Looking very carefully, she moved gently towards the puppy. As Mildred neared Marmalade, the puppy saw her and leapt on her and began licking her all over.

"I bloomin' love you! Let me help you regurgitate your food..."

Mildred miaowed in protest. Suddenly, Marmalade swiped at the playful pup.

"Stop it! Stop it at once!" said Marmalade.

The puppy pulled back.

"Eh? What's this? Good boy! What's this? This makes noise, is chewy, yes, you like? It best toy in world! Yes, c'mon! Good boy."

Marmalade lured the puppy away to the kitchen with a small, rubber dumbbell that was impossibly, brightly coloured.

"That's it! Right. In there... Good boy."

Slam.

The kitchen door closed.

"Idiot! Thank goodness for that. That chuffin' dog is not right in the head! And they wonder why cats are more superior.

"Right Mildred: I need your help. It turns out that the churches in the world have got it all wrong! Jesus wasn't born in December, no. The dude was born in September. The date is sort-of right but the month is definitely wrong."

"How do you know?"

"We've just been there. Anyway, I can't go into all that. Suffice to say, we have to do something about this and convey this mistake to those idiot humans. And on that, I'll hand over to Tinks, who has an ingenius plan."

"Right then," started Tinker. "When humans put the Christmas tree up and make it look nice, you must destroy it and bring it down. So when they put tree up, bring it down and spread the word to every cat, that Christmas is in September, not December, okay.

"This way, whenever they see us attack and destroy the Christmas tree, they will associate us with telling them Jesus was born i**n September**. A nota bene here though, if the tree is adorned in September, *that's okay*, fine, tickety-boo. Only if it's beautified in December shall cats destroy the trees. Pass this teaching on to every catlet and subsequent generations of catlets, for evermore and evermore shall it be."

And this is how & why cat's destroy and bring down Christmas trees in December.

Hidalgo residence, Cleethorpes, 16th May 1969,

One minute after High Tea

“Your coat, sir?”
“Yes it is.”
The butler, although slightly confused, moved back and directed the guest towards the reception room.
"Who are you?" asked the host.
"Why, don't you know?"
"Know what?"
"Well, I don't know what you don't know."
"I don't know who you are!"
"Allow me to introduce myself. My name is Twosugars, Detective Coffee Twosugars."
"Coffee Twosugars?"
"No, white with a sweetener, please. And you, Senor? Who are you?"
"But you came here! You came here and you don't know who I am?"
"I know who you are. The question is, do you know who you are?"
"Yes, of course."
"Good, good. If you would show me the precise location of the crime, please."

The host led Coffee Twosugars out of the room, through the hall and up the grand staircase. After a short walk on the landing, they went along a passage to a balcony that ran the length of the grand, old, stately home.

"Ah, a balcony. What a lovely balcony. And an amazing view! Such wonderful rolling hills and fields, painted like a canvas. My late grandmother liked a good balcony with a view."
"Oh, I'm sorry to hear that."
"That my grandmother liked a balcony with a view?"
"No about your grandmother's passing," said the host tilting his head slightly, in reverence to the departed.

"No, she's not dead, she's just late. Can never get anywhere on time."
"I see. So what do you think happened?"
"I'm guessing she never got the watch I sent her..."
"No, no. Do you think this is where the murder happened?"
"Murder, what murder?"
"Well, I presume it was murder, due to the blood on the balcony over there."
"Never presume, Senor. I presumed once and never again. No. What I am investigating is a missing person. I know a person is missing and that is all I know. Ah, over here I can see small traces of blood. Maybe they were struck over the head by a blunt object with a hard edge."
"Maybe."
"So we have a missing person with a head injury, possibly a concussion."
"So you dont think it was murder?"
"That, Senor, I do not know. What I do know is that somewhere there's a person walking around with a head injury, dripping blood and presumably concussed."
"I thought you presumed once before and you said, 'Never again!"
"Senor, never say never."
"But you just did."
"Yes, I know I did. Now, Senor Hildago, did you know this person and what was their name?"
"Yes, Audrey."
"Hmm and when did you last see Yes Audrey?"
"Sunday evening, about 9pm."
"Sunday at 9pm," the detective wrote down on his pad. "Can you be more specific?"
"Is 9pm not specific enough?"

"You can never have too much information."
"Well, I was watching the snooker on the television and was wanting a glass of port, so I wondered where Audrey was, so I called her..."
"Yes Audrey."
"Yes, Audrey, and asked her for a port. She brought me a sherry though, but never returned when I called her a second time, so I went to find her, but she had gone. I searched for her and as a result, came out here to the balcony, saw the blood and that's when I presumed that she had been either kidnapped or murdered."
"Yet it was not until this morning that you reported Yes Audrey as missing."
"That's correct."
"Hmm."

Senor Hidalgo led them off the balcony and back to the landing.
"Who else was in the house at the time?"
"Oh me, well, that's the wife and I, were in the living room, Mr Kelsey was up in the attic and Cook was in the pantry, I believe."
"And what about the butler?"
"Jives?"
"The butler Jives?"
"No, he is called, Jives."
"This jiving butler, where was he?"
"Well, I don't know."
"I see..."
"What are you thinking?"
"I'm wondering if the Goon show will ever return."
"How is that relevant?"
"Senor, how is it not relevant?"
"Never mind. Do you think the butler did it?"
"First, I have to check his alibi. Where is he?"

"I'm not sure."

They descended the stairs and Hidalgo summoned the butler to the living room. After a couple of minutes, the smartly dressed man arrived, with a stern smile on his face.

"And you are?" asked Twosugars.

"I am the butler, sir."

"The butler. What is your name?"

"The name's, Jives."

"How do you spell that?"

"With letters."

"I thought so."

Jives having faltered slightly, gave a gentle cough as a feint aroma filled the air.

"Are you well, Jives?"

"Not too bad, but I've recently started spontaneously defecating and it's rather painful. Things just spontaneously come out from my derriere."

"Oh, I'm so sorry to hear that. How long?"

"7 inches."

"No I mean, how long have you had it?"

"Up to 9 inches."

"No, how long have you had the condition?"

"Oh, I see - 2 years."

"But I thought you said it only started recently?"

"Well I'm 48, so 2 years is recent for me."

"48? I thought maybe you were younger than that..."

"How young?"

"Maybe 38?"

"38? And what size waist do you think I have?"

"What's that got to do with it?"

"Well, if everything to you seems smaller, maybe I could lose some weight. Umpf."
"Are you alright?"
"Forgive me.I need to change my underwear. Excuse me, sir."
"Oh you...."
"Yes, I'm afraid I did.".
"Oh, don't be afraid!"
"Alright; I courageously defecated."
"Can you courageously defecate?"
"Er, well my ol' behind is definitely not shy... not at the moment anyway," chuckled Jives.
"Anyway, where were you last night?"
"I'm an actor, so I was at the amateur dramatic society rehearsal. I am also their accountant. We were performing our last rehearsal before the opening night, which is tonight."
"I see, I see. What is the play called?"
"Hey Man, Don't Fall Backwards."
"A curious title for a play. And what part do you play in it?"
"In the play I play the part of the imposter."
"I see so you're pretending to be someone that you are not?"
"Yes."
"But surely, as an actor, you do that naturally?"
"No, that's just acting. In this play I am acting as an imposter."
"So who am I talking to now? The imposter, the actor, or the real you."

"Ah, but I'm all three..."
"So you are a butler, an imposter and an actor... how do you know which is which?"
"Ah, well, an actor is an imposter to fool the audience that I'm not me, but the character in the play is the imposter fooling the characters in the play, but the audience know I'm an imposter."
"So why dont the audience tell the other actors you're the imposter?"
"The audience doesn't interact with the actors in the play."
"Then how do you know they're there?"
"Because I can see them."
"Is it you that sees them, or the imposter."
"Both."
"Well, it's no wonder that actors often have mental health problems. Anyway, you must excuse my interrogation, please, don't let me stop you from going and changing your undergarments."

Intrigued by the butler, Twosugars decided to see the play for himself and ask questions of the other actors to verify Jive's alibi. In order to do this however, he needed the consent of the local Chief Constable, who would only allow this on the condition that he was able to escort him. The Chief advised that he would meet the detective outside of the theatre. He would be in plain clothes, wearing a grey suit and expecting Twosugars around 1945hrs.

That evening, Coffee arrived at the theatre and looked for the man in the grey suit. Spying a smartly dressed gent, he approached with due caution.

"The name's Twosugars, Coffee Twosugars. I'm looking for the Chief Constable."
"Well you won't have to look far."
"Will I not? That's good. How far?"
"How far for what?"
"How far will I have to look?"
"Well, only a few feet.."
"How many?"
"Er, four."
"Well I've got 2 and you've got 2 so he must be very close."
"He is. He's me!"
"Really? So you're incognito?"
"What?"
"You're incognito."
"No, I'm the Chief Constable."
"Nice to meet you. I'm Twosugars, Coffee Twosugars. By the way - if you ever go undercover I wouldn't go telling everyone who you are."
"I don't."
"Well, you just told me."
"But you thought I was incognito."
"But I didn't know who you were...?"
"But you do now."
"So are you being you now, or someone else?"
"I'm being me!!!"
"Right, then I'll be someone else. Who should I be?"
"Enough. I'm waiting for that idiot detective."
"Nice to meet you."
"So you're the detective?"
"Sssh, I'm incognito."
"Incognito?"

"Yes, incognito ergo sum - I think therefore I'm someone else."
"I thought you were Coffee Twosugars?"
"I am, but don't tell anyone..."
"Anyway, what's the time? The play must be starting soon."

Twosugars rummaged around in his pockets.
"What are you doing, Detective?"
"I have the time on a piece of paper... Aha, it's 7:55pm."
"But what if it's not that time when somebody asks you?"
"Then I don't look at the piece of paper."
"Oh, this is madness! Let's go in and take our seats."

The two policemen entered the theatre and had their tickets stubbed and then went to the bar for a drink, prior to the play starting. The Chief was not in the habit of suffering fools gladly and Detective Twosugars was making him suffer very much indeed. Moving towards the auditorium, they looked about for a suitable place to watch in comfort.
"Where are you going to sit?" asked the Chief Constable.
"On a chair. That's always best, I find."
"No, I mean, where?"
"Oh, I see. Over there."
"Over there? Behind the pillar? But you won't see anything..."
"Good, I don't want to see anything."
"Why ever not?"
"Well they say seeing is believing and I'm somewhat of an atheist when it comes to plays."
"You're an atheist viewer? Is that even a thing?"

"Yes. My mother was a atheist and my 2nd father an agnostic."
"Your 2nd father? What happened to the first?"
"I believe we never met."
"You *believe* that you never met? I thought you were an atheist?"
"Only part time."
"A part time atheist? What are you the rest of the time?"
"Anxious."
"Why anxious?"
"In case I'm wrong and God does exist."
"Anyway, what are we watching?"
"A play."
"Called?"
"Hey Man, Don't Fall Backwards."
"Hey Man, Don't Fall Backwards?"
"Hmm, that's sound advice."
"You're infuriating, you know that?"

The curtain was raised and the play started, allowing silence to descend and actors to begin. As the drama escalated, Twosugars left the auditorium and made his way backstage, so to question the actors and verify the alibi of the butler.

The dressing room was a hive of activity with make up being put on, outfits straightened, lines being rehearsed and excitement breeding like butterflies in the stomachs of all. As Coffee mooched about, he nodded, encouraged and made the acquaintance of the crew and cast.
"Excuse me, miss, do you know Jives?"
"Hidalgo's butler? Sure, yeah, I know him," said the young actress, looking Twosugars up and down.
"Was he here last night, at the rehearsal?"

"Sure. Why the questions?"
"Pardon me, my name's Twosugars, Detective Coffee Twosugars."
"How'd you get that name?"
"When my mother was in labour, she requested a drink. Soon after, I exited the womb as the nurse asked what drink she wanted, hence my name."
"Coffee Twosugars?"
"She actually wanted a Dry Vermouth, but the nurse said that they didn't serve alcohol, so she settled for coffee, with two sugars."
"Well, Detective, I'm Lulu le Boum."
"Lulu le Boum, eh? I bet you go off with a bang."
"Only if someone rubs me the wrong way."
"What happens if they do it the right way?"
"You wanna try, Detective?"
"Is that an invitation?"
"Maybe."
"How would I know for sure?"
"Well, why don't you try?"

Twosugars liked her. She was hot, so hot she could make steel molten by just looking at it, make an ice cap melt by merely giving it a glance and make a volcano's contents rush to the peak by simply breathing nearby to it. She was the kind of woman you didn't want to take home to meet your mother and father. The kind you'd hide away from other men due to the magnetic lure of her polarised features, yet she caused North to become South and South to rise Northwards with a wink of her eye. She knew what she was doing, even if you didn't and if you did know what you weren't doing, you certainly would've, but she would know about it before you even thought you'd have thought about it.

Admiring her, Twosugars took a match from its box and tried to strike it alight on Lulu, with no success.

"Well, that was more of a whimper than a bang."

"Don't try too hard, Detective. If you over think it, it may complicate things."

"I always under-think things, that's why my thoughts often overtake me."

"That doesn't make sense..."

"Does life ever make sense?"

"Only if you're an existentialist who enjoys crosswords."

"Okay, give me a clue."

"Four down, nine letters: Onomatopoeia."

"Errrrrrrrrr?"

"You're trying to hard again, Detective."

Leaving the policeman to figure it out, Lulu moved on towards the stage. Coffee continued in his quest to establish the whereabouts of Jives the night before.

"Excuse me, do you know Jives?"

"Who wants to know?"

"I do."

"And who are you?"

"The name's, Detective Twosugars."

"Is Detective your first name?"

"Coffee."

"Don't mind if I do."

"How do you take it?"

"The same way I like my milk; evaporated."

"Anyway, was Jives here last night?"

"Yeah, he was here, he was cooking the books as he normally does on a Monday night."

"Cooking the books eh?"

"It was like watching a lasagne being made from numbers."

"Uhuh. Lots of layers, you mean?"

"No, messy and covered in béchamel sauce. He was fine until that Audrey came in making a scene."
"Yes Audrey?"
"Yeah, Audrey."
"A scene, eh? And in a theatre of all places."

It all started to make sense to Twosugars now; Jive's faced two problems - fiddling finances for the amateur dramatics society and a meddling dame.
He obviously needed a solution to both dilemmas, but there was no proof and he needed hard evidence. Coffee called up the forensic accountants and arranged for them to inspect the finances the next morning.

At 10am, the team turned up and tore the theatre apart looking for the books, but it was no good, for Jives had them at the Hidalgo residence. So they went there to investigate further. They found them in the pantry, underneath the lasagne sheets and next to the béchamel sauce. The forensic auditor set to work. It was a tough job, like determining the ingredients of a Welshman's stomach; why was there so much lamb?
"What seems to be the problem?" asked Twosugars.
"I'm not sure," said the forensic investigator.
"You're not sure? Then there's no problem."
"But there is."
"What's the problem then?"
"Well, it appears that the figures don't add up..."
"Well, close your eyes and they'll disappear."
"But the figures don't add up..."
"Try multiplying them."
"They still still dont make sense."
"Try dividing them then."
"If multiplying doesn't work, the division certainly won't!"

"Maybe, but as they say, a problem shared is a problem halved."
"Do they?"
"Yeah, so share it with loads of people and the problem's sure to go away."
"Y'think?"
"Well that's the logic."
"What about their accountant, Jives?"
"All accountants are rubbish at maths."
"How you figure that?"
"Mine always says it doesn't add up and I tell him that's good enough for me. So hire 30 accountants and share the figures between them and the problem you have will gone away."
"That'll cost a lot of money though."
"Just hide it in your books and I'll get my accountant to go through them."
"What's his name?"
"Yes, that's him. You know him?"
"No. But anyway, that doesn't solve how Jives has fiddled the books."
"Well, y'know what else they say? If the fiddle breaks the bow, try a viola."
"I've never heard that before."
"You have now."

Armed with his evidence, Twosugars assembled the family and staff in the Hidalgo's reception room the next day. The silence allowed the ticking clock to be listened to, but not heard due to the noisy thoughts of suspicion and guilt. Coffee entered and walked about, hands behind his back, like a sergeant on parade.

"Now, I expect you are all wondering why I summoned you here," he announced.
"Well, I imagine it's to go through some lengthy preamble in which you deduce who the murderer is, then an even longer speech about why they did it," said Senor Hidalgo.
"Thanks for reminding me. Yes, one of you in this room IS the murderer of Yes Audrey. Therefore, one of you is Yes Audrey's murderer and of this you are guilty."
"But she committed suicide," announced the maid.
"How do you know this?"
"She left a note saying she couldn't go on any longer."
"Like my tailor..."
"Your tailor?"
"Yes. Poor man, he had a length of material that was too short and left a note saying that he couldn't make it any longer."
"You mean he couldn't take it any longer?"
"I don't know but either way he was coming up short. So you're saying there's no murderer? But a good way to get away with murder is to leave a note saying someone couldn't take it any longer and then say it was suicide. So maybe you're the killer!"
"Me?!"
"Yes you! Where were you at 12.15 on the 31st February 1956?"
"I don't know...".
"Then I accuse you of murdering my tailor!"
"What about the woman?"
"You want that to be taken into account as well? So you confess! I knew it all along..."
"No, I don't. And February only has 28 days, not 31. Maybe 29 in a leap year."
"Do you know my accountant?"

"What's his name?"
"Yes that's him. Do you know him?"
"Er, no."
"Umm, yet you know my tailor.... and both the woman and the tailor are dead. I conclude therefore, that you're the murderer."
"I'm the murderer?"
"Aha, you confess! I always break them down. Yes, I arrest you for the murders of..."
"But I've killed no one."
"Yet you just confessed. You all heard, didn't you so you're coming with me."
"But I'm innocent!"
"I thought that you're the maid?"
"I am!"
"Well make up your mind! Are you the maid or the murderer? Or both?"
"How can she be the murderer? There's been a suicide note left and Jive's was not here shortly after the blood on the balcony was found. Plus, Jives has motive, as he was cheating on his wife with her," interjected the bee keeper.
"And just who are you?"
"I'm the bee keeper."
"What is your name?"
"Mr Kelsey."
"And what do you do, Mr Kelsey?"
"I'm the bee keeper."
"Well, why didn't you say that in the first place?"
"I did!"
"Now don't be funny with me! And where were you the other night?"

"I was fumigating the loft to get rid of the Xestobium rufovillosum..."
"The what?"
"The Deathwatch Beetles."
"And you, who are you?" he asked the rather plump looking lady sitting by an occasional table.
"Me? I'm Mrs Ena Lilley."
"And what do you do?"
"I'm the cook."
"Senor Hidalgo, I should warn you that your cook has probably consumed most of your pantry, judging by the size of her. Anyway, Mrs Lillypad, where were you the other night when Yes Audrey was murdered?"
"I was listening to the radiogram in the drawing room."
"How very convenient."
"Well, it was actually, as I was tired and Fred McSpottin was came on the radio waves with his hour of music-hall delights, so I sat down and enjoyed the music."
Twosugars continued to pace the room.
"And last of all, Señora Hidalgo, where were you the other night?"
"I was here watching the snooker with my husband! And how dare you accuse me of being the guilty party!"
"I suspect everyone and no-one."
"Whatever do you mean?"
"I mean that no one suspects that I suspect everyone until my suspicions have been satisfied and I have found the suspicious person, or persons, being suspected as guilty suspects of the kidnapping."
"I thought was murder?" shouted Mr Kelsey.
"Murder? Who said it was murder?"
"You did!"
"When?"

"You said that one of us, 'in this room IS the murderer of Yes Audrey. Therefore, one of you is Yes Audrey's murderer and of this you are guilty," said Kelsey the bee keeper.
"I'm guilty? How am I guilty? I'm the Detective! You old fool!"
"I'm not saying you're guilty – all I'm saying is that you said it was murder, then said it's a kidnapping, when we all know she left a suicide note saying that she couldn't go on any longer. She was having an affair with Jives the butler, who was fiddling the drama society's books to keep his wife happy in the manner she'd become accustomed to, whilst he was knocking of Audrey."
"Yes Audrey?"
"Yes, Audrey!"
"Now look here, are you the detective?"
"No, I'm the bee keeper!!!"
"Enough!!! I've had enough of this! There's death watching the beetles in the attic, a bee keeper who thinks he's a detective, a lily who eats everything, a maid who confesses to a murder she hasn't committed and a butler who makes lasagne out of books whilst having affairs with Yes Audrey! AND people wonder why there's dysfunction in families these days! You are hardly setting a good example now are you? No!"
"So, who is responsible?" asked Señora Hildago.
"Society, I believe Señora. Society, that is whom."
"No, you idiot, who killed Audrey?"
"Yes Audrey?"
"YES AUDREY," shouted everyone.
"Oh, I confess, I confess. I can't take any more of this," said the butler, Jives, who broke down in tears and pleaded for mercy.

"I knew it!" said Twosugars. "You thought you had just rectal problems, well, my friend, they're going to get worse..."
"Then why on earth have we had to put up with this nonsense?" enquired Senor Hidalgo.
"Because, like you said, Senor, I have to, 'go through some lengthy preamble in which I deduce who the murderer is, then an even longer speech as to why they did it.' And now, Jives, I arrest you for the kidnapping & murder of Yes Audrey, for acting as an imposter and cooking number lasagne, of which I'd very much like to try a morsel at some point."

Jives was then arrested and taken to the police station by Twosugars, who was fired the very next day by the Chief Constable.

Earl's Court Underground Stn, UK, 4th October 1911,

Around Morning Coffee time

"What we need is a gimmick."

Stationmaster Jones patrolled the platform, spying the escalator each time he passed it. This was the first mechanical staircase ever to be installed at an underground station in Great Britain. It was great innovation that kept Britain being great, but no one would use it. No, not one person and this is why the stationmaster was in the throes of deep thought.

"Taffy, would you be so kind as to perambulate this mechanical stair system for me, please?"

"Nah, no, nope, not never. It'll eat me up and spit me out!"

"Now that sort of comment does not inspire confidence in your employer. In fact, it indicates your lack of enthusiasm for this venture. We need someone to use the blinkin' escalator, so to encourage others to use it. If an employee of mine fails to utilize the facility of these perambulatory steps, it does not encourage others and members of the general public to use it either. So Taffy, if you would be so kind."

Taffy looked at the contraption and took one hesitant step on it. It started to move, which caused a nervous reaction, meaning Taffy's foot retracted from the escalator.

"I don't trust it!"

"Believe that it will escalate you to the dizzy heights of the vestibule and it shall be so. Place your faith in these steps, Taffy."

However, Taffy was a man of little faith and great doubt. He looked upward towards the entrance hall, whilst shaking his head in a negative manner.

"No, nope, never. Get someone else."

Taffy walked away along the platform towards the steps

and marched upwards.
"If I may," said a small voice. "What we need is people to see how safe it is with someone on it."
"Er, yes. I do believe that you are correct in your assumption and that is what the present dilemma is. Contrary to your observation, I have been trying to motivate candidates to use this facility, and that is why I presently have no one to partake in a mutual exchange of experience on the said equipment. Right as you are, this has been most foremost in my thoughts, with no lack therein, yet your observation of the most obvious conclusion is indeed the dilemma which vexed me. Worry not, that this idea has been captured in my mind's eye, for I can assure you that it is most foremost within the sphere of my consciousness. In conclusion, I am fully aware of this need, without the aid of your most obvious perception."
"Sorry, of course you are. I have an idea though," replied the young lady.
"Might it be that you have something constructive to say? Or is the input of an obvious nature as beforehand?"
"It's constructive."
"How wonderful," said the Stationmaster, in his bookish, nasal, sarcastic tone.
"I had an relative who was a stunt performer in the talkies..."
"Let me stop you there, Annie. You indicate that you had, 'an relative, who was.' May I point out that we need a living person to volunteer, not a deceased one. Inasmuch as I appreciate the dead may be willing to participate in this exercise, we do, my dear, need a very much, living participant."
"They are alive, I can assure you. Bill was a stunt performer and if you pay him a shilling, I'm sure he'll

oblige you."

Jones looked upwards and approved of the idea. Arrangements were then made for Annie's relative to come to the underground station.

Later that day, around 1400hrs, Bill turned up at the entrance hall of Earls Court Underground Station, with his niece, Annie. Stationmaster Jones approached them with a broad smile, which diminished more with every step he took towards them.

"Good day to you, Bill, isn't it?"

"That's right. I'm Annie's uncle. My name is William Harris, but everyone calls me, Bumper."

"Yes, I can most assuredly assume that they do."

Jones looked Bumper up and down, noticing that he had only the one leg left, which was coincidentally, the left one.

"Annie, I now understand why you used the past tense upon referring your charming uncle, Bill."

Annie looked sheepish and bowed her head as an apology to the omission she had made.

"Has Annie explained what is required of your good self, stipulated the necessary steps required?"

"She has indeed. You want me to use that escalator thing, so to build confidence in its construction and mechanical reliability."

"Yes, this is what I most certainly require. A role most suitable for traditionally, a two legged person. Not that I'm at all prejudiced against monopoled persons."

"Well, I am a qualified stunt performer. I've been performing stunts for many years now, in moving pictures as well as the talkies."

"So I hear! Begging pardon of my possibly foolish ignorance, I am curious as to know how you lost the faculty of your lower right limbs."

"You want to know how I lost my leg?"
"Yes, indeed. I am intrigued by how a successful stunt actor such as your good self has become deficient of a leg."
"I was in a boating accident."
"In a war presumably?"
"No, Actually it was at the Cockney's Henley in Battersea Park."
"Well I never! I had literally no idea that nautical leisure activities were so fraught with danger. In Battersea Park, you say! My, my! Well I never, indeed!
"Forgive my curious nature, Bill, but I am enthusiastic to know how you endeavour to navigate the underground station and the escalator."
"Well, I just hop on and hop off."
"Hop on and hop off.' What a profound answer you have to the escalatory conundrum I perceive. Yet, what if, God forbid, the hem of your trouser should get caught within the edge of the mechanical steps? How would you escape?"
"Well, I'd just stay in the centre of the step. Safer that way. You need me to walk up and down the escalator?"
"No, Bill. That is not required, for the perambulation of the mechanical steps is sufficient to guide persons both up and down the said elevator, without need for individuals to feel the necessity to amble. For this is the sole purpose of the aforementioned equipment, so to save their vehicular motor functions and enable the graceful movement twixt the vestibule and platform, the transit of which is the escalator, being the medium that is used for this facility."
"Okay. You're not worried are you? I'll be fine."
"Me? Worried? Never. That thought is farthest from my mental anxieties, Bill. It is the public I'm concerned for, as

when they see a handsome, rugged, one legged man, such as your good self, on the escalator and possibly perceive the notion that you lost your leg on your first venture upon the moving stairway. 'Ooo, I wonder how he lost his leg?' they may enquire and consider how such a catastrophe occurred. So I am inclined to label you with a sign bearing the legend, 'lost leg at Battersea.' And hope that no one hunts for a sole, wooden appendage at the Battersea Park lost and found department. Yes, we shall label you accordingly."
"Okay. Shall we get started?"
"I admire your enthusiasm, Bill."
"Call me, Bumper, as everyone else does."
"To be honest, Bumper, if I was to see you circumnavigate the escalator and call out from the platform, 'Bumper, my good man,' I fear two potential problems may occur. One, that some husbands may inadvertently believe that I am encouraging them to bump their wives down the stairs whilst in motion, which may result in calamity and two, that people may assume that you, an admittedly one legged man, have the pseudonym of Bumper, which is not necessarily a positive nickname to call out when members of the public are travelling alongside you. No doubt they will look for you and discover a unidexter, albeit a handsome one, in the midst of them and their unified thoughts will be, 'A one legged man, named Bumper? I hope he is not named as such due to his monopole nature! Hmm, I better not stand next to him, lest he inadvertently bumps into me!' Thus causing mass panic in a public transport environment.
"Now where was I?"
"I was asking, should I get started going up and down the stair thingy?"
"Hmm. Bill, I do admire such enthusiasm, I really do,

however if the passengers frequenting the establishment happen upon the scene of a single legged man, vigorously hopping up and down the escalator, they may think, 'That's odd; why is a solo male, who is bereft of a limb, persistently hopping on and off the bloomin' escalator? Surely the staff do not employ a physically challenged person to perpetually travel to and fro on this perambulatory stairway.' And with this in mind, I think we shall set up an event whereby you, William 'Bumper' Harris, are the star attraction, displaying the safety of the new escalator technology for all to see. Is that alright?"

"Yes, that's fine!"

"Brilliant, well see my secretary and we'll set a date so to promote the safety inherent in our technology and your good, stunt performing self. Nice to meet you, Bill."

Tiflis Meteorlogical Observatory, Russia, April 18th 1916, 1805hrs.

Newsreader: And that was the news at 6 o'clock. Now we have the weather with, Joseph Stalin.

Stalin: Good evening. There is a warm front approaching from the North-East which is bringing the rain, rain... the reign of Nicholas the Second to an end!!!

Director: Er, Joe? Just the weather please. The weather only, okay?

Stalin: My apologies. It will be a damp and warm night, due to the oppression, the er, the oppression, yes, the oppression of the Romanov royalty!!! It will end, will end!!! We will bring down the royals!

Director: Joe! Joe! Joseph! Please... This is a weather forecast, not a stage for your Marxist commentary! The weather, please...

Stalin: Forgive me. There is a warm front approaching from the North-East, making it a warm and damp night. The early morning will see the wind rise, oh.... Oh, there's two little cats here, here in the studio. Hello, little cats.

Cat #1: Good e'en to you. My name is Marmalade and this is m'colleague, Tinker. I was wondering if you could help me: are you any good with crossword puzzles?

Director: How did those cats get in here?

Cat#1: You wouldn't believe me if I told you. Now, Mr Stalin, you're an intelligent, if not somewhat misguided, man. I wonder if you can solve this crossword

conundrum.
What has five letters: is not dissonant, musically, yet like a Mandarin or Cantonese – last letter is an L?

Stalin: Er, I'm not sure...

Director: Get those cats out of here!

Cat #1: Sir, I understand your distress at the sudden appearance of us cats, but would you kindly desist from shouting. Mr Stalin, your answer please...

Stalin: What has five letters: is not dissonant, musically, yet like a Mandarin or Cantonese – last letter is an L? Frankly, I have no idea. Anyway, what do you mean by saying I'm misguided?

Cat #1: All I'm going to say is, I understand that you want to usher in a more industrial style of agriculture, but think of the poor farmers. You can't leave them high and dry, for they rely on their land, cattle and harvest for a living, and I fear you may become a bit (what's the word?) over zealous with your urge to modernise the infrastructure of agricultural society, as much as it might need dragging into 20th century.

Stalin: How did you know? I'd like to explore your ideas about farming.

Cat #2: Nevermind all that. Marmalade, your seriously close to breaching the time travel code of conduct.

Cat #1: Pity, as I wanted to share my ideas around pest control and farming with Mr Stalin. Anyway I bid thee a good evening.

Stalin: Where did they go?

Director: Where are they?

Stalin: They've simply disappeared!

Director: Anyway, Joseph, the weather, please

Somewhere in Tibet, 18th August 1260,

Just after afternoon tea

"It's chuffin' cold here, Marmalade!"

A temple covered in snow stood before them in the mountains. A yak clanged its bell as it drearily sauntered about.

"Well, she looks happy," said Marmalade as he noticed the dour look of the beast.

Making their way towards the temple, they noticed a few horses loitering near to an archway that led to the inner compound of the building.

"We'll go in here, Tinker, and get shelter.

Leaving tiny, gentle paw prints in the snow, they progressed through the courtyard and along the hallowed pathway. The building seemed so vast to the cats, looming over them, making Tinker feel like it was going to topple on him as he looked upward. Eventually they discovered a suitable entrance and made inwards to what seemed to be a holy room that had benches and richly coloured walls of gold and red. Deep blues emanated from jewels located in the rails, statues and icons of assorted heroes and saints were scattered all over, making the large temple a whole lot smaller.

At the center of the floor stood a well weathered chiseled Mongol, dressed in rough but tailed animal skin with thick fur trimmings. He wore a hat that made Tinker and Marmalade chuckle, being a small leather dome surrounded by thick, black and grey fur. On top of the leather dome was a piece of red wool about two inches long, with a fluffy pom-pom attached. The Mongol walked around what appeared to be a holy man of the highest order, who knelt

before him trembling in fear. Two other Mongolians dressed in a similar fashion to their boss, stood by two large ornate doors, stopping any entry or exit.
"So, what will it be? Do we have to kill all of you or will you accept our rule and pay taxes to your new leader?"
"We will never be ruled by anyone, nor pay taxes. We are but humble monks, seeking a peaceful life."
"You are arrogant and disrespectful of the Khan! I will destroy you all if you do not allow us accession over your land. Step down, accept the Khan's hand and pay taxes."
"We will never..."
"I have another idea," said a voice that seemed to be hiding a body somewhere. Out from the benches, came an older, bald priest, wearing a thick linen robe and a waistcoat made from some short-haired animal.
"And what is your idea, old man?"
"Tell Kublai Khan that we can make sure his name and lineage will go on forever. We will allow his rule of our land, serve him, and assure succession of his rule for future generations. Pay taxes we cannot, for we ourselves are poor. What we do have is what I offer now."
"And just how can you do that?"
The older priest moved closer, smiling gently and bowing his head reverently.
"There is reincarnation and we help discern who returns to this realm, not escaping samsara. As we discern, we can persuade others to understand just

who has returned. This influence, we have."

The Mongol narrowed his eyes and pondered over the suggestion. He walked around the hall, stroking the ornate ornaments, statues and gem-crusted rails. "I see you are very poor indeed!"

The Mongolian bodyguards laughed as their leader indicated the irony.

"They are worthless. To you they appear like rich ornaments, yet they have no value to one who believes not in Bon and the Buddha. Where you see wealth, we only see wisdom, for they help the believer focus on the power represented by the icon. Likewise, we can enable those who believe the Khan will return to rule, help them seek the Khan in his new guise when he departs this life, so his most gracious wisdom will remain to rule his bountiful empire, of which we will surely help him to rule. Our treasure is not material but of another realm and worth more than rubies, sapphires and precious metals. Offer this to the Khan and I shall personally assure him secure succession of his rule over his entire, growing empire."

The Mongol thought about the words being said, pacing as he did so. The two cats were watching from nearby and hadn't been noticed as yet, thus were enjoying the unfolding drama.

"And how can you do this?"

"Well, like I explained, with reincarnation priests & monks are frequently asked to *help* discern who successor shall be. So, we could, *assure your* succession by carefully discerning your ancestors, so to continue the Khan lineage."
"I like that! It truly is worth more than 'rubies, sapphires and precious metals.' The Khan agrees."
"It will be so."
The cats looked at each other, aghast.
"Tinker, what an utter swizz! That's terrible! How could anyone do that?"
"Those who are worried about losing their life?"
"That's cheating in my book! Anyway, I think we've seen enough here – come, let us continue our travels."
And with that, they disappeared from sight.

Somewhere in the desert, Sinai Peninsula, 1268 BC,

Early morning

After many years in captivity, serving as slaves under Egyptian rule, the Israelites have wandered the desert in search of home. Facing many hardships, they are led through adversity and the desert by their fearless leader, Moses...

Aaron: Got a minute, Moses?

Moses: Why, what's up?

Aaron: There's someone who wants a word with you.

Moses: Let him come in...

Reuben: It's about the food.

Moses: What about the food?

Reuben: When are we going to get some?

Moses: Did you miss breakfast?

Reuben: No, I had breakfast, but we want to know when we're going to get some proper food.

Moses: Are you saying Manna isn't proper food?

Reuben: No, but that's all we ever eat now; Manna.

Moses: What's wrong with Manna?

Reuben: Well, nothing, but we have it every day, twice a day.

Moses: Oh, I see, ungrateful are we?

Reuben: No, it's just we have Manna all the time and nothing else!

Moses: Well, be inventive, try making new recipes with it!

Reuben: But we have! We've had manna rissoles, manna on toast, roasted manna on a bed of manna, manna with a side of spiced manna, manna & chips, a surfeit of manna on a bed of curried manna, manna sausages, fillet of manna, manna chops with freshly boiled manna & a slice of manna bread and a cup of tea, boiled manna in a habanero sauce, sautéed manna, manna fingers, diced manna Provençale on a cartouche of manna nicoise with a manna sauce; grilled manna, compote of manna with a crème manna béarnaise, chipotle manna with fresh tortilla of manna, manna guacamole with manna salad and manna pate. We have eaten manna every bloomin' way possible.

Moses: How about steamed manna on a bed of manna fingers?

Reuben: We had that last Thusday.

Moses: Oh, right.

Reuben: We're getting sick of blinkin' manna! Manna for breakfast, manna for lunch, manna for high tea, manna for supper, manna for brunch.

Aaron: We have had it a lot Moses...

Moses: You shut up. How about using that lettuce we found the other day?

Reuben: Are you mad? Three lettuces between 36,000 Israelites! There was barely a leaf each! Even then you said, "to bulk it up with manna," and spread it thin! All we're eating is manna. We want to go back to Egypt where there were cucumbers, herbs, spices, bread, meat, fish, pickles, preserved fruits, fresh dates, olives, sesame oil and those little, preserved dill pickles with mustard seeds in the vinegar.

Moses: Nah, we ain't goin' back to Egypt. It was an oppressive society where we were ruled by a tyrant who propagated a fascist regime, thus making the bourgeoisie the elite.

Reuben: But we liked that fascist tyrant and at least we got fed....

Moses: You are getting fed!

Reuben: Only flippin' manna! We're only eating manna! Manna with this, manna with that, manna with the other...

Moses: So you're telling me that you actually liked working slave labour, under a hot sun, getting whipped and beaten with rods and badly managed by a false elite? You actually liked that?

Reuben: Well, yer kinda get used to it, don't you? I mean, what's a bit of slavery between friends? And my wife, she loved a good lashing now and again! Moses, let's go back.

Moses: Nah, I'm not having it. And if I ask God, you know what He will say, "It's Yah's way or the highway!" And I know where my road is marked and which way to go.

Reuben: But we want to go back, have something decent to eat...

Moses: Well, of course, it may be a bit difficult now as well – remember the chariots and charioteers, let alone the horses, that perished in the waters of the Reed sea? They'd hold that against us. We'd be held accountable for the loss of those soldiers. Then there's God: He might think you lot are being ungrateful. Fresh manna ain't good enough for the Israelites, eh? Oh, no they want pickled dill pickes and fresh herbs! "Would you like some manna?" – "No, I want fresh fruit from a despot who treats immigrants as slaves, coz manna ain't good enough for me!"

Reuben: Well, actually, maybe you're right...

Moses: Uhuh... How about some prune juice? Want some of that too? Freshly oppressed by a dictator? Or figs: how about a fascist fig? Communist cucumber anyone?

Reuben: No, I understand your point. Maybe we'll try manna roulade? Or maybe entrecote manna moues bouche....

Moses: Yes, that's the spirit.

Heaven Inc., 7th Epoch of Eternity,

Coffee break

"No, I'm not doing an interview with Piers Morgan! You can tell Janice that I've simply tonnes to do! I'm getting quite frustrated y'know with all this, er, this stuff going on. There's always something to do and things to organize since this rebranding shenanigans. Why did we have to 'move with the times?' Things were fine as they were. Now it's, 'we need to enhance the customer interface,' or, 'Can we facilitate this incentive with positive export?' I mean, what does 'positive export,' actually mean?"

"I believe it means, can we hurry things along. Can I be of more help maybe?" asked Doris, trying hard to be helpful.

"Dear, sweet Doris, I'm afraid not. It's just part of the job. Being God is not always easy y'know ..."

"How about asking the Archangels to help out more?"

"No, good grief no! They're overworked as it is! I'd just be giving them more opportunities to say, 'Yes, of course I will,' but see that facial expression which actually says, 'Do I have to do it, really?"

"Well just explain everything to them.... Or maybe have a word with that nice Dr Jung, talk it out and get everything off your chest."

"Doris, my dear, I'm supposed to draw people to my bosom, not get them off of it. What would people think?"

"I'm sure Dr Jung would treat it with strictest confidence."

"Yes, actually he probably would. Unlike Freud, gossiping about the place and saying I have 'issues' with my father. I have no father, or mother, I just Am, so it doesn't make sense! A bit like when the blooming focus group ask me to, 'reprise the viability of the expedient option.' What on earth does that mean? It's pure gibberish!"

"Dr Jung would definitely be the better option, I think. Just go and see him!"

Doris said it in a way that was sympathetic yet almost

patronizing, wrinkling her nose and narrowing the eyes behind her glasses. Taking a sigh, God thought about her idea and that it might actually be a good one. Considering this, God's lips sort of chewed the idea, contorting the facial expression until a decision was made.

"Right, I'm off for a bit. See you later."

Carl Jung was sitting in one of the celestial parks, watching the ducks meander over the pond. The water was perfectly translucent and one could see the universe go about its business by watching through it. A duck waded across the watery window, creating concentric ripples over a galactic supercluster. The peace and tranquility was delicately disturbed by God appearing before him.

"Can I borrow you for a chat?"

"Why, of course!"

Sitting down on the park bench, God placed his left arm along the top of the bench's back. Carl adjusted his seated position, so to open his posture and face his client. "How can I possibly help you?!" was his thought, but it came out vocally, in a rather surprised manner.

"Oh, I don't know! It's all just getting on top of me!"

"What is?"

"Everything."

"And everything is...."

"Getting on top of me."

"Yes, I understand that; I'm looking to understand what this 'everything' is though."

"Well, it's just..... everything. Have you seen the amount of emails I get? Prayers? Texts? Do you know my prayer to blessing conversion rate? 1.01%! That's excellent, the best it's ever been!"

"Conversion rate?"

"Oh its since we've 'rebranded.' It's out with Heaven Inc.

and in with Bliss. We've now got a statistics team, a focus group which, parenthetically is more like an out of focus group, a think tank, a marketing team and an image augmentation force. All these things aimed at making my job easier."

"What's an image augmentation force?"

"They design the corporate image of Heaven, sorry Bliss, as well as maintaining my customer intervention facet."

"Customer intervention facet?'

"It's a new way of saying, public image; how people see me. "

"This all sounds very good, but not you."

"What do you mean?"

"The terms you're using sound corporate, like think tank, marketing, conversion rate; that's not your voice. It's not you. Your words are more, more poetic, free and simple."

God made a silent single chuckle.

"You're absolutely right. That's Janice speaking not me."

Dr Jung matched his posture to mimic God's. Leaning slightly, he considered what he was about to say very carefully.

"Maybe it's time to change things. Go back to as things were, as opposed to keeping up with the trendy version of Heaven."

"Bliss..."

"Yes, sorry, Bliss. You're talking like a businessman, not God."

"Or maybe I should get out of this line of work. Do you have any idea how many complaints I get? People moaning about why something happened, or crying out, 'What made you do this?' and cursing.... Then there's the complaints. Yesterday alone, I received 6.7 billion complaints! Then there's people shouting, 'Oh, god," or, "Good lord!" I mean, are they asking for my help, or just blaspheming? It gets very confusing when you hear your name mentioned every few seconds. And it makes you paranoid.... Are they talking about me? Or are they talking to me?"

"I think you need a break..."

"I did that before, but I got pestered all the time; mobile phone kept ringing....."

Carl smiled gently and took time to construct his prescription.

"Well, you either need to make some changes or, like you say, change your line of work."

God thought about it silently for a few moments. Looking at the transparent pond, God noticed another spark lighting up in a nebula and a comet wending its way through a star system. Could God really hand over the reigns to someone else?

"I used to enjoy the old times; the odd visit, nipping down there to see what's going on, have a good ol' natter, inconspicuously moving about and talking with people. It was simple then; no marketing strategies, no conversion rate targets, no product placement. No 'adding value.'"

God even used virtual apostrophes to emphasize the term.

"Well, I'd seriously think about what you would do."

And with that, God said, "Thank you" and disappeared from view.

As God arrived back at HQ, Doris was busy rearranging the schedule due to St. Peter having to go and greet some guests earlier than expected.

"Doris, come in here, my love, please. Bring your jotter with you as well."

Doris flustered about then quickly left her tasks and entered the office where God now sat behind the large desk.

"Take this down, would you: Wanted, Chief Executive. No scratch that, most of them are wanted by the police anyway. Er, how about, General Operations Director required. Bliss, requires a General Operations Director to take over operations in a corporate eternity, to start ASAP. Must have experience in the nonsecular environment. Despots need not apply.

"You will 'be,' and be working in a fast paced environment, delivering an exceptional end-to-end customer service experience. Being used to a high pressure and a high performance work ethic, your skills will be enhanced within the business, as will your decision making skills.

"Ideally, you'll be a team player with the ability to work within a trinity and as an individual, encouraging all to go above and beyond; to achieve and maintain crucial performance levels and enhance morale in a demanding environment. You will be leading our first class team as we deal with complaints, prayers, delivering blessings and miracles, delegating as appropriate and communicating changes to senior stake holders and partners.

"Desired skills: an enlightened mind, negotiating, ability to cope well under pressure, experience of an ethics committee, able to achieve KPIs, empathy, have a forgiving attitude, omniscience & computer literate.

"Essential skills: effective communication skills, sound listening skills, use of Mac based software, calm and positive "can do" attitude, understanding of teleology & "cause and effect," to be "as is," Quantum mechanics, exceptional knowledge of cosmology.

"Preferred skills, but not essential: educated to Doctorate standards, ability to move quickly (in mysterious ways), omnipotence (but we can train you), ability to smite (as required).

"A full background check will be carried out. If you feel you have the skills, we provide fantastic rewards: full relocation package, use of company vehicle, unbeatable life insurance policy, use of refectory, free Halo and gown; salary is negotiable for right candidate, and subscription to our on site gym!

"Full job description available on request. Work for Bliss and you'll be on cloud 9. Send your CV and cover letter to Michael@bliss.org.

"How's that sound?"

Doris finished scribbling and then let a tear fall from her eye and navigate over her nose.

"Your not going somewhere are you?"

"I don't know yet, but I want to put the feelers out and see if there's any suitable candidates who could do my work and lighten the load somewhat."

God noticed her tears and went to console her. Placing a friendly arm around her shoulders God reassured her that it was no fault of her own and that God was merely considering retirement.

"You do stirling work my dear. I wish I had more like you to carry out the good work we do, I truly do. You have nothing to be worried about."

"But I like working with you! What if the person you hire is a complete incompetent?"

"Then they'd be consciously incompetent. Takes a lot of skill to be a leader as well as a professional idiot, as Donald Trump has proven. Anyway, remember, I am with you always. Now let's get the advert out there and see who bites."

As soon as had the advertisement been placed on the ethereal noticeboards and on the internet, a barrage of applications swept in to St Michael's inbox, thus enlightening him to the job opening and that he was in charge of sifting the wheat from the chaff. Applications came from both the corporeal and eternal realms. After some extensive filtering, the aspirants were shortened down into a shortlist, which was again shortened to a shorter shortlist.

"It's like a celestial 'Britain's Got Talent," said Michael as he perused the names.

"Well, I don't believe I Am is holding auditions for the role! Heaven forbid! Anyone can act godly, but being godly is another thing altogether!" said Raphael as he peered over Michael's shoulder to read the names. "Have you seen some of the résumés on here? Arnold Schwarzenegger?'

"Oops! Get rid of that one..."

"Friedrich Nietzsche?"

"Maybe not..."

"David Hasselhoff?"

"Er, how did he get on the list..."

"Kubla Kahn?"

"Big oops! Yes, of course I've seen the names on here. Anyway, I best get this over to the Lord straight away!" said Michael, as he removed the name, Walt Disney, then sent the list, with the respective Curriculum Vitaes attached, via email.

Doris opened and printed off the email as soon as it arrived, knocked on the office door and waited to be invited in.

"We've got a list of prospective names for you to have a look through."

God accepted the printout, looked at it once, then curtly asked Doris if she could summon St Michael, as swiftly as she could, which she did at once upon leaving the room. St Michael walked in promptly, humming the Hallelujah Chorus. The look on God's face indicated that something

was wrong, halting the tune on Michael's tongue.
"If this is your idea of a short list, I'd like to see who you'd install as successor!"

God stood up and walked around to the front of the desk and stood almost face to face with the archangel. "So, come on, talk me through it, as I'd just love to know your thinking. Who's first...? Let's have a look shall we; Richard Nixon, so this is a good start! Why him?"

"Well he applied and looked good on paper," said Michael, trying unsuccessfully to find some personal space. The ensuing silence brought a stern gaze from God.

"Next is Buddha! Are you having a laugh? Is this all a joke to you?"

"Well, actually it's as he explained it himself on the additional comments section; people worship him, which kinda defeats the object of what he preached, so he thought he might as well apply. Fancies his chances."

"Who's next? Jimmy Carter. Well, that one's not too bad I suppose. Ah, this next one confused me. It just says, Pope - which one? As there's been quite a few."

"All of them."

"All of them? What d'you mean, 'all of them?"

"All of them."

"What all at once?!"

"Each of them applied, individually, as it's the promotion they were all looking for, natural progression and all that..."

"Then this one I don't understand... Chur-something? The predictive text has misspelt it. What is it? Chinchilla?"

"No, it's Churchill, Winston Churchill."

"Hmm... Next we have, Confucius."

"Yes."

"If he got the job we'll all be eating horse meat and he'd insist we write everything down, lose it, then try to

rewrite it! Things would take an eternity! Who else.... Ah, interesting one; Akhenaton. Why, pray tell?"
"Well, he got the main concept right about monotheism and wasn't too bad a ruler, he likes cats, and looked good on paper!"
"David Beckham?"
"Nice chap. Great ideas, gives to charities, fantastic football player."
"Here, I think that you're thinking about the forthcoming interfaith football match aren't you! So, which of the disciples would you bench when we play Nirvanorg in the Celestial Cup?"
"Probably, Thomas, as he doubts his ability."
"Let's see who's next shall we.... Joseph Stalin. Joseph Stalin!?! Are you mad, Joseph Stalin?"
"Well, actually, he seemed very keen!"
"I bet he did....! Next? Mark Twain, possibly, but too much of a smart Alec. Er, then we have Socrates. Why Socrates? Are you thinking about football again or the philosopher?"
"The philosopher. He asked if a theocracy could truly be a democracy on the application and I liked that."
"He's just being clever, plus if he got offered it, he'd decline it. Ah, now please explain this one to me, Michael, please as I'm really trying my hardest to understand this one, Jean-Paul Sartre? For heaven's sakes!"
"Yes, that's right, Sartre. Clever man is Sartre..."
"He's an existentialist for goodness sakes! You can't have an existentialist ruling eternity!!! Kind of defeats the object, don't you think? Eh? Next there's, Emperor Hirohito."
"Be looked good on paper also..."
"Margaret Thatcher?"
"Wasn't many women on the list...."

"In the part about, 'what changes would you make?' she writes that she wants to privatize and outsource most departments!! What's wrong with you! Then there's this lot, Zeus, Aphrodite, Hera, Poseidon, in fact the whole bloomin' pantheon! What's got in to you Michael?"
"I was just trying...."
"Trying to what? See who could fail at the job so badly that you'd get promoted? Know your place! Who's next, eh? Who's this? Ah, we have Oppenheimer, he who quoted the Bhagavad Gita, 'Now I am become death, the destroyer of worlds."
"He's looking for a second chance and looked good on paper...."
"Second chance? Are you mad? We'll all be blown to smithereens! Then we have, Martin Luther which one?"
"Both."
"What at the same time?"
"No, each independently applied, of their own volition."
"And why on earth is Kim Jong-Un on here??"
"He seems confident he can do the job and looked..."
"'...looked good on paper?' René Descartes?"
"Ah, now that's only as long as we don't allow animals in to Bliss, as it would negate part of his philosophy."
"Constantine?"
"Well, he is a visionary..."
"Lao Tsu?"
"He'll do the job, but he states he'll only do it his way or no way at all."
"Queen Elizabeth I?"
"One of the few women who did apply."
"Albert Einstein?"
"Great 'ideas' man."
"He may well be, but eternity is no simple thought experiment! And this one, Mike Myers? Who on earth is

Mike Myers?"
"An actor, did the voice of Shrek and played Wayne in 'Wayne's World' He said he, 'always fancied playing the role of god; would be helpful method acting for him, as he wants to expand his repertoire."
"Alanis Morrisette?"
"She enjoyed acting you in the film, 'Dogma' and thinks she'd be good at it."
"Hilary Clinton?"
"My apologies about that one, that's an honest mistake.."
"Interesting one here; Robert Kennedy?"
"Very keen indeed and he has the full support of his family."
"That's as maybe, but something always happens to a Kennedy... Lucretia Borgia?"
"Er, interesting ideas around food and reformation."
"Good grief no! Schrödinger?"
"Nice chap. Another one who's a cat lover; wants to prove something about existence...."
"Germaine Greer.... Heaven forbid! No, no, no. Now then, here's an interesting one, Krishna."
"He wants a full role as deity as opposed to the part time role, which he currently holds."
"Michael, Michael, Michael.... I must say I'm a tad disappointed. I mean, why isn't the likes of Gandhi on here, or any of the disciples?"
"Ghandi didn't want to apply. He did say, however, that he'll go on a thought-strike if you decide to retire."
"Thought-strike? What's on earth's that?"
"Based on the idea of 'I think, therefore I am,' he'll stop thinking until you comeback as the G.O.D. (It's the nearest equivalent to a hunger strike up here, you see)."
God looked disappointed, walked back to behind the desk and sat down in the executive styled swivel chair.

"I was kind of hoping St Paul, Ghandi, Mother Theresa (bless her), or someone like, oh, I don't know, Florence Nightingale would apply! Not the likes of," God paused and looked over the sheet of paper, "the likes of Robert Maxwell, Genghis Khan and Joan Rivers!"
"Well....."
"Well what?"
"There was someone, a complete unknown; we think he accidentally applied for this when he was actually applying for a night shift shelf stacker for Alfa foods stores...... Name's Jordan Lightfoot."
Michael handed a piece of paper over the desk to God, who took the proffered leaf and read it.
"Good grief no! I don't think he fits the bill, do you? Hobbies and interests: Watching Family Guy and gannin' oot an gettin' drunk on Saturday nights?"
"Well, what are you looking for in the aspirant?"
"What do you think? Good sense of the moral maze, sound judgement, works within the spirit of the law, smites only when totally required, knows how to tweak the cosmological constant when necessary; someone who's inventive and creative; someone who knows people, and is good with them. Someone who lets everything have its chance and encourages ideas, strengths, et cetera. Oh, and does a lot of good work for charity."
"Well I know, just the person. They'd be ideal and they're the only candidate in my eyes...."
"Who?"
"Well, you!"
"Me?"
"Yes, you!"
"But the whole point in this was to find someone to train up who could eventually take over the reigns!"

"There is no one like you though, Lord."
"Of course there are! There's stacks of them down on Earth alone! I didn't create them in my image for no reason y'know!"

Then God paused and thought for a moment. An idea whirled about the mind and Michael could see the cogs of the Almighty turning.
"You know what? I'm going to ask everyone to help. I'll give them faith and when two or more come together to decide on things, and if they agree, it will be done."
"Is that such a good idea? Shouldn't there be some sort of buffer just in case they decide on something peculiar, like, er, like.... all residents of Kendal to be called, Mintcake; Tuesdays must be on a Wednesday, except for when there's an 'r' in the month; Britain must not be able to leave the European Union; compulsory wearing of marzipan hats for bald people; benefits for people with high fringes; tax all ginger haired people called Mildred; food that goes off at midnight should be placed in a bomb shelter; Celine Dione to be dissected and spread over the four corners of the world; soap operas must bring back dead people in a plot to bring them out of unemployment; Simon Cowell to audition potential Prime Ministerial candidates live on TV or, or, all rabbits should eat marshmallows? I mean, it wouldn't be a good idea as rabbits can't stomach marshmallows..."
"OK, right..."
"Then we'd get an influx of people asking, why people are force feeding marshmallows to rabbits?'
"Yes, I get your point."
"Just think of all the complaints..."
"Alright, alright, I've got the point! Okay, so if two or more people come together and agree on something, and it's vetted by me, then it'll be done. How's that sound?"

"Sounds fine. I was just concerned as we get a lot of complaints, plus Moses and the legal team would go bonkers, as they do; 'Why's God said this? Doesn't God realise we have to underwrite these things..."
"Yes, yes I get your drift. Humanity hasn't fully realised the gravity of faith and their full potential. We'll have a word with someone who can wake them up a bit, make them see how mighty faith can be. It can move mountains y'know!"
"How about Oprah Winfrey?"
"Good heavens, no! Neither Deepak Chopra."
"David Icke?"
"A definite no! Someone who is brave, fearless, knows the tremendous power of believing 'it is done,' rather than 'it might be."
"Uri Geller?"
"That spoon bending buffoon? Not a chance! Anyway, I'll have a good think on that as I need to have a word with Janice now.'

God called Doris, in and asked her to invite Janice from marketing over, due to needing to, "have a word with her." As God waited for her to nip across, a smile formed on God's face and the peace was felt in the building of Bliss HQ.
"You wanted to see me?"
"Ah, Janice! Good to see you. Right. I'm making some changes around the place..."
"Well the focus group won't be happy..."
"Yes, the focus group, what can I say about the focus group; they're so out of focus that they can't reach back far enough up their bottoms to adjust the lens! Then there's that marketing team who want me to be like, er, I don't know, a doll that a child plays with and dresses it up in whatever fashion they see fit. I've had enough of all

that nonsense. I am who I am, and that's it! And they want to remember that!

"And no more of this modernization regarding concepts and terms! It's forgiveness - not soul cleansing; it's redemption - not S.P.I.F, all that sins paid in full acronym nonsense, it's redemption, plain and simple! And as for grace, it IS the pits!; it's not Positive Independent Temporal Space, it's simply grace; and I think I've been gracious enough with that! Well, no more, I tell you!

"I've had it up to here with people trying to 'reinvent' me. Next thing you know, they'll be trying to rename me as something peculiar like, er... Wise Holy Omnipotence.."

"What?"

"No, WHO."

"Who?"

"Me, that's who! I've had enough. Maybe I need to be a bit more Old Testament and start smiting people again; I haven't had a good smite in ages! So there, I'm putting my foot down."

Silence filled the room and Janice looked like a pupil who had been chastised by a headmaster.

"I'm sorry for having a rant but it needed to be said. I don't need to know my prayer to blessing conversion rate...."

"It's at its best ever 0.9%....."

"That's great, but it's not necessary! So, hopefully we can move forward from this and return to the simpler, traditional way we used to do things. As the man said, 'if it's not broken, don't fix it.' So I'll do my thing and you lot can can quietly do your own.

"There's too much dumbing down, analysing and tiptoeing around the obvious. There's a place and time for it, but it's not now. However, I do like the new name, Bliss, and that's what it should be up here, bliss, not an augmented re-enhancement of parallel eternity for sentient souls seeking peace. I mean, in that phrase alone, there's 10 words replacing one, Heaven. It is what it is, but like I say, I do like the new name for Heaven, Bliss."

Things were off of God's chest now and God sat down in the executive swivel chair behind the large desk as Janice left the office, feeling more peaceful and content. God called Doris into the office.

"You'll be happy to know that I'm not retiring after all."

Doris smiled and went back to work.

Neuskarsgarra, 15th February 3118 AD,

Mid-morning Coffee time

"And furthermore, we should annex the galaxy of Tripplethwaite before the civil war happens, so we can increase our troops."

The Grand Invigilator nodded his head in agreement.

"Yes, go and take our best envoys so to curry favour with the Tripplethwaites. And don't take no for an answer."

"Yes, Grand Invigilator."

The silvery-blue console moved allowing the ruler to stand up and walk his guest to the door, which seemed to dissolve, allowing exit. The long corridor glowed an iridescent blue and white.

"Excuse me" said a voice.

The Invigilator looked around but saw nothing.

"Hello?"

Still he saw nothing.

"Down here."

Looking downward, he saw two pussycats sitting near his doorway.

"We're rather lost. We were heading for Saturn moon-base Alpha Ypsilon, but lost our way somewhat. I was wondering if you could grant us advice on how to get there, please."

"How on earth did you two get here?"

"I'm not going in to all that now. I just need to know how to get to moon-base Alpha Ypsilon, if you don't mind. It's just we're pressed for time."

"Okay, it's, it's back down the corridor, turn left and carry on for about 2 kilometres, then you'll see the signs."

"Thanks ever so much, old chap, much obliged. See, I told you we should have turned right at the oligarchy headquarters..."

"Hang on..."

"Sorry?"

"How did you get here? Animals haven't been transported in this part of space for at least 200 years, since the flea infestation of Galactus Prime."
"Oh, we, we have diplomatic passports. We're on a diplomatic mission; we're boarding a federation ship."
"If this mission you're on is a diplomatic, then where are your ambassadors?"
"Allow me to introduce ourselves; this is Counsellor Tinker of the Trade Federation and I am Ambassador Marmalade. We are from the cat colony on Deep Space 13 point 5."
"What are you doing here?"
"Oh, we stopped off for a snack and to use the litter tray."
"Where are you travelling to?"
"Oh, that's on a need to know basis."
"Is it now. Well, I need to know."
"Can we trust you?"
"Of course. I am the Grand Invigilator, after all."
"Doesn't mean I can trust you! You might be a spy for the, the P'Tah..."
A curious look came over the Invigilator's face.
"The what...?"
"The P'Tah! I bet you are, aren't you? Tinker fetch the binders; we're taking him with us. DAMN! I knew it was a bad idea coming here..."
"I'm not a spy. I've never heard of the Pertarv."
"The P'Tah! It's them that have promised rule over the galactic central to the Perkinians. We are on a secret mission, under diplomatic papers, to see if we can stop the P'Tah from giving supremacy to just one race. Can we trust you?"
"Yes, yes! Like I said, I am the Grand Invigilator."

Marmalade looked about then led them to the Invigilator's room.
"Right then. Here's what I need you to do. I need two tins of Catty Chunk-Chunks, Herring flavoured, delivered to room 623 in precisely 15 minutes. Then you must go and sift through the litter tray in section Gamma. In there you'll find the Todmordern Capacitor..."
"The what?"
"Pay attention! I shall say this only once. I need the Todmorden Capacitor, so bring it to me in room 623, whilst we're eating the Catty Chunk-Chunks. Bide your time! And keep a look out for the agents of P'Tah."
"Right."
"Do you have a can opener?"
"What?"
"Do you have a can opener?"
"Er, no... No. I don't know what one is, or what it looks like."
"Uhm. That's going to be a problem. I need you to find one and bring it to me, urgently."
"What does one look like?"
"Look it up. Come, Tinker, we must leave quickly."
Then the cats left the room and went down the corridor. The Invigilator looked up a can opener on his computer as he called through to get two cans of Herring flavoured chunks for room 623. Feeling completely confused, he sat down to process the information.
As the pusscats traveled away quickly, Marmalade said to Tinker, "Well, the humans of the future seem to be as gullible as those of the past! At least we shall have something to eat before we move on from here. Now where's room 623... And I forgot to ask if he knew the answer to my crosswordpuzzle..."

Galactic HQ, SpaceFort 8, 4268 AD,
About 3ish

"General, I have terrible news."
"I know! It's been troubling me all morning."
"Has it, sir?"
The lieutenant stood to attention, awaiting the order to stand easy. General Hugo Porteus however, was frantically looking through drawers and files, cupboards and everywhere.
"Yes, Lieutenant James. It's been troubling me a great deal."
"So what are your orders? What shall we do?"
"Purchase some more!"
"Begging your pardon, sir, but purchase more what?"
"Underpants."
"You're going to thwart the Chottle by buying more underpants, sir?"
"No, no, no. I need more underpants! We're not going to defeat an army of significant proportions by using underpants, are we?"
"Absolutely, sir."
"No! No one, anywhere, ever won a battle with underpants!"
"No, sir."
"Unless, of course, they weren't wearing underpants, which would mean they were unprepared! An unprepared army is one without underwear on! They're the easiest battles to win. My first victory was against an enemy who failed to wear undergarments! They were very unprepared. A victorious army always has a decent pair of pants on... and warm socks too."
"Absolutely, sir."
The lieutenant was relieved, to put it mildly. He relaxed his stance and began walking around the room.
"What are we going to do, General?"

"Uhmmm. That is a very good question, James. But first of all, we need to find out where they are going."
"Absolutely, sir. If the Chottle are amassing on the planetary border of Galzon and attack, it will leave no doubt that they intend to take over the galaxy."
"No, James. I meant, where are my underpants going?"
"What?"
"Where are my undergarments going? That's the question. Or who is taking them..."
"Sir, I need a decision from you now."
"Very well, James. Take this down; now listen here, you Chottle! Bally well buck up and leave the region, or we will have to cancel the touring theatre production of, Strange Nights, by Atilla Smythe! Let that be a lesson to you!"

Lieutenant James looked confused, as well as in despair.
"No, no, sir!"
"You don't think that's harsh enough?"
"With all due respect, sir, the Chottle are heinous, despotic, warmongers!"
"Right, hmmm.... Ah! Take this down, James; Now look here, you Chottle. You must withdraw soonest, or we will subject you to a severe ticket reduction for the Gilbert and Sullivan Operetta simulation."
"No, no, no! We need to do something a lot harsher and decisive."
"The virtual reality world of Simon Cowell?"
"No, no, NO! Sir, we need to send a strong message letting them know we will act and retaliate."

The General thought and paced about to aid his rumination. After some silence, the General squinted and spoke.
"How about; I know you've been thieving my underwear and require its return posthaste, otherwise you will be

subjected to severe sanctions meaning, a distinct lack of roll-on deodorant and sanitizing toiletries , which will render you the smelliest alien race in the galaxy!"

"General, General, sir! Please! If we don't stop the Chottle, there wont be any underwear at all, or toiletries, or complimentary soaps, razors, moist wipe-ettes, anywhere in the galaxy, at all!!!"

"Heaven's no! I shan't allow this! Launch an attack, send in the troops, gather the Intelligence and reconnaissance: let's smash the Chottle!"

"That's more like it, Sir. We need to send signals and other communications to the outlying units."

"How do we do that?"

"From the signal station."

"Where's that again?"

"Just up from the socks and pants distributor, in Delta section."

"Ah, I know it well. Let's get going..."

Eldern Street, Middlesbrough, 16th April 2004,

About 10ish

Mitzy the kitten was not like other cats. She was shy, timid and not a natural hunter. Whereas most cats could catch mice, rats and birds, Mitzy did not have this inclination. Except there was one thing she was very good at catching and eating...

The other felines watched her as she would go back and forth between there and here, then play with something and then eat it. It looked like she was chasing and playing with nothing. It looked so odd and the other cats mocked her and made fun of her.

"What are you doing?" asked a cat, who watched from nearby.

"Hunting flutterflies," she said.

"Hunting what?"

"Flutterflies."

"Don't you mean, butterflies?"

"Nope. I mean, flutterflies."

"But there's no such thing as a flutterfly!"

"Oh yes there is!"

"No there isn't! You're just playing with thin air and making up nonsense!"

"No I'm not. And I'd advise you to start catching them too, for they can be very, very scary and be extraordinary big."

The other cat shook its head and walked off, as Mitzy cleaned her paws. She then wandered off to find more flutterflies.

After a while, the other cats became curious about where she was going to and from, so one of them followed her. Down the garden path it went, over the fence, along the field, under the hedgerow and in the hollowed trunk of an old tree. Nervously, the cat entered the tree trunk, but Mitzy could not be seen. It was very, very dark in the large trunk, and the cat looked up to the

murky top of the tree's innards, noticing something, but not being entirely sure as to what it was. So the cat began to climb up the inside of the tree, slowly, not being very sure-footed in this unfamiliar tree. Higher and higher it climbed, inch by inch, creeping and crawling, becoming frightened at the slightest noise, sudden movements and unrecognizable sounds. Then something flew past the cat's head, then another, then another, but the cat could not make out what it was. Then more flew close to its head and one landed on its face, covering the cat's eyes.
"Aargh!!! Aargh!!!" screamed the cat, as it fell to the ground and skiddadled out of tree. It ran to under the hedgerow, along the field then leapt over the fence to land in the back garden, screaming all the time.
"What is it? What is it?" asked the cat called Horace
"It's.... It's.... It's a... Fer, fer, fer, ffflll, fffhhh, flutterfly!"
"A what?"
"A fffff, flutterfly!!"
"What does it look like?"
"A big, black, fluttery fing with giant wings... It's 'orrible!"

Horace thought for a moment then asked the cat where it was. So the cat lead Horace down the garden path, over the fence, along the field, under the hedgerow and in to the hollowed trunk of the old tree. Nervously, the cats entered the tree trunk. It was very, very dark in the large trunk, and the cats looked up to the murky top of the tree's innards, noticing something, but not being entirely sure as to what it was. So the cats began to climb up the inside of the tree, slowly, not being very sure-footed in this unfamiliar tree. Higher and higher they climbed, inch by inch, creeping and crawling, becoming frightened at the slightest noise, sudden movements and unrecognizable sounds. Then something flew past their heads, then another, then another, but the cats could not make out what it was. Then more flew close to them and some landed on their faces, covering the cat's eyes.

"Aargh!!! Aargh!!!" screamed the cats and they fell to the ground and skiddadled out of tree, ran under the hedgerow, along the field then leapt over the fence to land in the back garden, screaming all the time.

"What is it? What is it?" asked the feline known as Fiona.

"It's.... It's.... It's a... Fer, fer, fer, ffflll, fffhhh, flutterfly!"

"A what?"

"A fffff, flutterfly!!"

"What does it look like?"

"They're big, black, fluttery fings with giant wings... And they're 'orrible!"

"Show me..."

So the cats lead Fiona down the garden path, over the fence, along the field, under the hedgerow and in to the hollowed trunk of the old tree. Nervously, they entered the tree trunk which was very, very dark. The cats looked up to the murky top of the tree's innards, noticing something, but not being entirely sure as to what it was. So the cats began to climb up the inside of the tree, slowly, not being very sure-footed in this unfamiliar tree. Higher and higher they climbed, inch by inch, creeping and crawling, becoming frightened at the slightest noise, sudden movements and unrecognizable sounds. Then something flew past their heads, then another, then another, but the cats could not make out what they were. Then more flew close to them and some landed on their faces, covering the cat's eyes.

"Aargh!!! Aargh!!!" screamed the cats and they fell to the ground and skiddadled out of tree, ran under the hedgerow, along the field then leapt over the fence to land in the back garden, screaming all the time.

"What's with all this hullabaloo?" asked Mitzy, sitting in

the sun in the back garden.
"We fer, fer, fer, found the fer, fer, fer, ffflll, fffhhh, flutterflies!"
"The what?"
"The fffff, flutterflies!!"
"What do they look like?"
"They're big, black, fluttery fings with giant wings... And they're 'orrible!"
"Uhmmm. If only you knew someone, or something, that could catch these flutterflies, eh?"
"Mitzy? Would you..."
"Would I what?"
"Would you catch the...."
"What? Catch a cold? A fly? A train, or bus?"
"Go and catch the flutterflies," cried all three cats.
"Oh, alright. I suppose so..."

So they all went down the garden path, over the fence, along the field, under the hedgerow and in to the hollowed, old, tree trunk. Nervously, they entered the tree trunk which was very, very dark. Three cats looked up to the murky top of the tree's innards, noticing something, but not being entirely sure as to what it was. The cats began to climb up the inside of the tree, slowly, not being very sure-footed in this unfamiliar tree. Higher and higher they climbed, inch by inch, creeping and crawling, becoming frightened at the slightest noise, sudden movements and unrecognizable sounds. Then they stopped, felt the flutterflies flying and fluttering around them. In the feint light of the tree they saw a huge object coming towards them. It was Mitzy, who had climbed up the outside of the tree and leapt downwards, inside to catch the flutterflies from above.

The cats scarpered, ran out of the tree, awaiting Mitzy, who casually sauntered out from the trunk minutes later, licking her lips and with her tail triumphantly flexing in the air.

"Thank you, Mitzy, thank you," said the cats and they never teased or taunted her again.

Freeman residence, Seaham, UK, 29th August 2018,

After 1130 am

"What are we doing here, Tinker?"
"Well, you want an answer and I figured, why not ask the author?"
"That nitwit?"
"Yes, him. The nitwit."
"The nitwit, idiot author who can barely string two or more words together?"
"Yes, the nitwit, idiot author incapable of placing a sequence of words into a sentence."
"Hmm, good idea actually, Tinks."
The long haired, Persian puss and his grey and white, time-travelling, tabby partner marched down the path, along the drive and hopped over the fence to find a rear entrance, as the backdoor tended to be the best location for cat-flaps to be fitted Tinker had discovered and he was absolutely right. How many flaps have you seen on front doors? In a porch maybe? But nine out of ten times it was located at the posterior of the building and it's here that they found it and walked in unannounced. The long kitchen was aptly lit for the time of day, allowing a dog cage to be seen, cat-scratching posts, a small sofa and the usual benches, table and cooker.
"Good grief, looks like they're trapped in the 70s! That wall paper is atrocious and who puts black and cream tiles on the wall! Now where's that bald buffoon?"commented Marmalade as they moved about the house. Tinker commented that the decoration was called, 'retro,' as they ventured towards the living room.
On the black, reclined armchair, the author sat having a snooze, his bald head reflecting the light and belly sticking out like there was a wok badly misplaced under his top.

"Oi, you! Author bloke! Wake up."

Marmalade sat on his chest licking the upper lip and nose of the writer.
"What the... Get off, man!"
The cat stopped licking and moved in a circle then sat on his host's belly with a stern grin on his face.
"Now listen here - I've got questions for you and you're going to bally well answer them!"
"Oh, it's you, Marmalade."
"Yes, 'tis I and m'colleague, Tinker. He's presently using the latrine, hence the lack of his physical presence. Now then, what are you playing at, eh? Giving me crossword puzzles that no one can chuffin' guess, eh?"
"Er, I wasn't aware I had."
"Then, why pray tell, am I forced to visit you and sit on your belly, viz à viz, asking you this question? Eh?"
The author started stroking Marmalade's long hair, rubbing behind the backs of his ears and then continuing long strokes of the fur again.
"Well, you like adventures, don't you?"
"Maybe... Stop stroking me! You're trying to trick me, by relaxing me so my guard is down, then bam, that's it! Another part of my anatomy will disappear, won't it? Like it did last time. I woke up in some awful metal, sterile cage with the smell of faeces lingering next to *Autumn Breeze* scented candles, in that veterinary practice, realising I was now un chat sans petit carotte, wasn't I? Yes!"
"Sorry, Marmalade, but it was necessary."
"Necessary? I'll tell you what is necessary baldy-wok-belly man, an answer! Now, tell me, what has five letters: is not dissonant, musically, yet like a Mandarin or Cantonese – last letter is an L?"
"Well, I don't know."

"What do you mean, you don't know? You wrote it!"
"That may be, but I haven't written *that part yet*, so haven't looked up and researched the question in order to write it. At this point in time, that you have visited, *now*, and are presently in, I've not written much save the initial ideas and what the book is going to be about. In my life you are a pet, but in my mind, your literary character has only lived for just a day and I am still developing you. So in a paradoxical way, you have inspired me to write that question as part of your story, moreover, your quest. So really, you should know the answer, due to you asking me a question I haven't yet asked!"
"For pity's sake! So I am the author of my own dilemma! Well, who in earth will know the answer?"
"Good grief, I haven't a clue. Someone clever, obviously. Er, Stephen Fry, Stephen Hawking..."
"Anyone named Stephen, then," said Marmalade, as he rolled his eyes. "And whilst I'm here, I want to know something: what's with making me go through every possible, bizarre combinations of words and sounds to find the name of those blessed aliens? And the ridiculous scenarios you place us in - why? What's got into you? Are you insane?"
"Well, firstly, I am sane and secondly, you're a sort of tulpa."
"A tulpa? What's a chuffin' tulpa?"
"You're a creation of mine, that I give free lease to. Even though your creation, to me, is relatively recent, I aim to let you navigate your own story and explore your own experiences."
"I thought that I was a cat!"
"You are, but also a tulpa."
"This is all very odd, if you ask me. All I want is a relatively easy life, a bit of adventure and some of Mrs Fortescue's

home grown catnip now and again, but now I suddenly find that, although a pet & evolved, I'm also a mere babe comparatively and sound like a song by Gene Pitney."
"A song by Gene Pitney?"
"Yes, 24 hours from Tulpa. And I, so it would seem, have orchestrated my own dilemma! What bizarre paradox is this that vexes me? Oh, can anyone solve this crisis? I need to know!! I need to Know!!! "
"Know what?"
"You really are a dithering numpty, aren't you!? I need to know, what has five letters: is not dissonant, musically, yet like a Mandarin or Cantonese – last letter is an L."
The author thought about it and then said, "God would know."
"God ***will*** know. Considering you're a writer, your grammar is absolutely terrible, but you are right, God will know.
"Come, Tinker. That is where this bizarre paradox will be broken. Let us go post haste to the very beginning of everything..."

Somewhere in the cosmos, -10 mins prior to the birth of everything

"Tinker, we're no longer in Seaham," announced Marmalade as they looked about at where they were. It was like a vast void and what appeared to be nothing was all around them. Marmalade noticed Tinker looked different, he was glowing and like stardust, but he recognized him still as who he was. The tin can time machine was fine though, still intact, its little lights flickering.

"Why, you look different, Marmalade."

"So do you. Thankfully the time machine is still as it should be. Where are we, Tinker?"

Looking at the machine he said, "Apparently we're 10 minutes before the big bang, but I can't place the location..."

Marmalade thought for a moment, then realised where they were.

"Tinker, we're nowhere dude. Nothing exists yet. That's why we look so different. That means the Supreme Cosmic Being should be around somewhere..."

Amazed, Tinker started fiddling with the tin can, in a metaphysical way, for his paws were now different and had no physical form. In the distance, something began to travel towards them. It was small and luminous, yet indistinct. Nonchalantly, it sauntered in their direction, taking it's time and whistling. The sound caused a quizzical look on Marmalade's face.

"What's that dude whistling? I seem to recognize it... is it 'Magic Moments'? I believe it is.

"Excuse me, hello! You over there... Stop whistling and come here. Yes you."

The noise stopped and the thing began to come closer. Then it stopped travelling and suddenly appeared right in front of them.

"Hello, would you mind telling me where we chuffin' are? I have an appointment with the groomer at noon tomorrow and need to get back sharpish."
"Oh, there's no tomorrow, not yet anyway."
"Another thing, why do Tinker and I look different, and who exactly are you? Or should that be, what exactly are you?"
The formless cloud of light chuckled.
"Er, Marmalade, I think that this is, this is..."
"This is what? Some sort of cosmic warehouse? An industrial estate somewhere in the universe? We're obviously in something, but as to what, I'm unsure..."
Tinker stopped Marmalade.
"Marmalade, I think this is the SCB."
"What this little, glowing ball of light?"
"Yes."
"Well, are you?"
There was a pause and from somewhere in the depths of the cloud they sensed a smile.
"Oh, something like that. I'm not sure you'd completely understand who or what I am. I just am."
"What kind of answer is that? Are you unsure as to whom you are? Do you need therapy to help 'find yourself' as those Americans call it?"
"No, I don't need therapy, I know what I am. I'm just me."
"Oh, is this some Zen Koan or something?"
"No, it's no puzzle, it's just me being me. I was wondering if you would like to hang on a bit and watch the birth of your universe. Everything, well nearly everything is in place. I'm just missing one thing... Ah there it is..."
The being lured the tin can time machine towards itself, as a pair of cosmic hands mysteriously appeared. Seeing the being and tin can together broke a memory within Marmalade's mind.

"It's the... it's the... It's the hands for the cans in the vast expanse!!!"
"What?" asked Tinker.
"In the beginning were cans in the vast expanse, then there were hands for the cans in the vast expanse!!! Tinker, this is the SCB! The Supreme Cosmic Being!!!"
"Er, yeah. The readers and I already got that."
"You're a lot smaller than I thought you'd be."
"I get that a lot," said the SCB.
"And why of all things, do you need our tin can time machine to help the universe get kickstarted?"
"Well, at the moment, everything is going to happen all at once, so I need time. It'll be a gift, a present and this present will help things know why they exist and answer those questions I get asked all the time: what's it all about? Why am I here? Why is there this? Why is there that? If I give things the gift of time, the present, they'll begin to understand.

"So, right then. I'm gonna start the universe now, so is there any place in particular that you would like to exist?"
"Twenty-first century England, please," said the cats instantly and unanimously.
"But not near Basingstoke! Bloomin' awful place. The bus service there leaves a lot to be desired," quipped Marmalade.
"Somewhere near home," said Tinker.
"Okay then. I can do that. I will also allow you to ask me one question, one only mind, as I know that whenever things meet me they always have questions. So think about it and ask."
"I got this," announced Marmalade very quickly.

Tinker looked at him very quickly and said to the supreme being, "Excuse me, er us, one moment..."

The two celestial cats pulled back slightly and had a

discussion.
"Tinker, trust me, dude, I got this. I know the question we need to ask. It's been vexing us for ages and I'm pretty astute and know you would want the answer as well."
"Are you sure? It's not going to be something stupid is it, like a lifetime supply of Cheeky Chunks or Jerk Herring? Or a self cleaning litter tray? Or an eternal catnip bush? Invisibility? Eternal life?"
"Good grief, no! I'm not an idiot, Tinker, not like that bloomin' author bloke! I'm not going to ask for something stupid - trust me."

The cats humbly approached the Supreme Cosmic Being, Marmalade smiling wisely and calmly.
"The question we have is this; what has..."
"Oh no..."

Tinker lifted his head up in despair.
"What has five letters: is not dissonant, musically, yet like a Mandarin or Cantonese – last letter is an L?"

There was a pause, then a prolonged silence. Finally, the SCB spoke.
"You could ask me absolutely anything, yet you want me to solve your crossword conundrum?"
"Yes, dude. I'm a simple cat with simple tastes; I like Cheese flavoured Cheeky Chunks, a bit of Mrs Fortescue's catnip, and kibble now and again, yak milk and, of course, crossword puzzles."
"Okay Marmalade. The answer is, Tonal."
"Of course it is! Tonal. Tonal. TOE-NAL. That's great dude, thanks ever so much. Tonal, how about that then!"

The Supreme Cosmic Being then took the tin can and began to open it with two conveniently crafted, cosmic hands and then poured out the time machine's ingredients into the universe, looked at it, smiled and said, "That's good. Now, brace yourselves..."

How it all began...

It was a chilly, autumnal afternoon in early June, when I rather fancied some cheesy flavoured, Cheeky Chunks, but there weren't any. So I had to settle for some Pilchard flavoured Jerk Herring instead. The manufacturers should have fished the Atlantic side of the waters, then it would have been Sardine flavoured, which is even better. Anyway, there I was, flicking my tail in jest, whilst lounging on the living room floor watching the laborious role of some woman on the televisual set. She was in some sort of soap opera, that the humans love, but they bore me to tears I can tell you; all that drama like, Sharon's got her knickers in a twist about Kev's latest girlfriend, whose hamster has conjunctivitis, which seems to mean it can no longer use connectives like 'and' in sentences. Parenthetically, I've never heard a hamster speak – no, not a word, especially after I bite its wee little heady off. Anyway, these soaps are absolutely ludicrous! Now there's this stupid bint, Kyra, whining on about how Ty isn't paying her attention anymore; it's no bloomin' wonder, with all that b*tch*ng and complaining she does. I wouldn't be paying her attention either, no! I don't blame him for seeking solace with Rae down the road at number 42. And what's with that idiot, Lefty Flatfoot; he's a blithering idiot! He can't string two or more, er, things, yer know (what they called?) words, that it, together, no he cant can't string two or more words together, no! Then he tries and means well, but he's just an idiot. I mean, really... Who thinks that thieving the Christmas Fund money to pay for his neighbours kidney gender reassignment is a good thing? And who in their right mind thinks that, that posh bit, Teena, really loves you? She's using you, you fool, can't you see that? No, obviously not, no. Idiot, he is.

Anyway, I do digress.
Where was I?

Oh, yes, on the living room floor having eaten the Jerk Herring. I also happened to be doing a crossword puzzle in the newspaper. The Sudoku was simple, but the crossword was causing certain perturbation.I had got 2 down and 5 across, but 12 across was being a real challenge, I can tell you. It vexed me greatly. So I opted for another clue, 17 down – Liquid, it might be either – which was, Ore. Then 8 across was, Lack of enthusiasm causes inhibitions to be squandered – Unambitious, but 12 across still bit me. It was then that m'colleague, Tinker, popped over. He's a bit of a whizz with technology, always tinkering with things, hence his name.

Anyway, we were rudely and forcefully adjourned to the dining room, due to the pater of the house entering and sitting down, then turning the televisual thingy over to the football match, where his team would no doubt lose again and the rants would begin about how Jiminez should have been played left back, "as in left back in the changing room," the goalie should "wear glasses" and, "read the ball better." I could swear the chap's missed his vocation – he should have played all the positions in a one-man-team against any adversary. He also should have been the referee, who bore the brunt of much abuse, of which I dare not write down. This so-called expert should be out there doing everything on the field, not working as a data processing nitwit at the local abattoir.

Where was I?

Oh, yes, so Tinker and I adjourned to the dining room, the crossword in my paws. Tinker asks if we have any tin cans around the place and I point him in the direction of the recycling box.

Off he goes and I'm stuck on the bally crossword conundrum and now listening to the radio quiz-type program that frequently airs called, That Ain't No Moon, It's a Space Station. It's a veritable mix of comedy and factoids of information that has Andy Hamilton exercising his wit on one side and that buffoon, Amil Atatürk, on the other side, making smarmy comments that ports to be comedy. He gets on my nerves, he really does. The wife of the house likes the show and laughs at his feeble puns, which shows she does have a sense of humour after all. (I think the biggest joke in her life is the obvious one she married several moons ago!) I agree with her mother, that he's an ignorant, chauvinist, swine who'd be better off working as a navigator to those devoid of common sense and decency, as he's always telling people where to go and how to get there, very impolitely.

Anyway, she was laughing at Amil's anecdote about how he once had a dog that couldn't catch its own tail (like I'm bothered!) Tinker was tinkering with tin cans and I was trying to continue with my crossword, when I thought, "What if we could circumnavigate time & space?" I often muse over such things and gave voice to my thoughts by telling Tinker. He thought it a brilliant idea and stated that he was, coincidentally, working on a time travel device after finding some mathematic function on a piece of disposed paper. Apparently it resolved an issue regarding Perturbation Theory and the formula that Tinker was dealing with took this aspect in to consideration when bridging 2 points in time, with the help of Heisenberg's Uncertainty Problem. Apparently, now, Tinker could locate the location and velocity of a body in motion, within the fluidity of space-time and utilize quantum tunnelling to bridge these two aspects.

I told him, "I don't understand all that, I just want to traverse time." It was at this time that he revealed to me that he used work for the CIA. Yes, amazing isn't it! I was astounded. He says that during the formative years of the Cold War, he was a cat especially trained for Project Acoustic Kitty, which consequently became a multi-million dollar failure. However, his tip-top-secret training had equipped him with a certain skill set – he was now a genius. A genius in what exactly, I don't know, he keeps that under wraps, I can tell you. What I do know is that his genius most *certainly isn't* in common sense; who in their right mind would invent pussycat pants for incontinent cats? Really...

And then there's the time when he tried melting the cheese on to the toast by placing the cheese in the toaster with the bread. He never lived that down! They're still scraping the stilton off of the ceiling now. There was camembert every bloomin' where and you could smell burnt toast from Haxby Grove to Windywilly Lane (Don't snigger. Everyone sniggers when they hear that name.) So in short, Tinks is gifted, definitely, but not all of his faculties are blessed in equal measure.

Anyway, where was I?

Oh, yes, we were talking about us cats potentially travelling through time. So Tinker, inspired by the idea of mine, starts converting the formulae of temporal mechanics into a device that can thrust us through time. Eventually, he solves the problem, that has dogged humans for years, and invents this time machine thing, then with the help of his former CIA colleagues, we sort adventure and peril by travelling through time. Together, Tinker and I embraced the annals of space-time, history and the future, having many marvelous encounters on the way.

A note from the author.

These stories, aided by Marmalade, are designed to preserve some lesser known moments from time, as well as preserve the classic comedic styles. You may notice the echoes of certain comedians & writers as you read. It is not intended to be an infringement, but a tribute to them. It's important to cherish and hand down these skills and styles so they will live on. So, Marmalade and I, salute and honor you.

Bud Abbott & Lou Costello*
Harold Lloyd*
Stan Laurel & Oliver Hardy
Groucho Marx*
W C Fields*
Mel Blanc*
Peter Sellers*
Spike Milligan
Michael Bentine
Leslie Nielsen*
The Pythons*
Sir David Frost
Leonard Rossiter
Ronnie's – Barker & Corbett
Bob Monkhouse*
Bruce Forsyth
Kenneth Horne*
Kenneth Williams
Peter Cook* & Dudley Moore
Eric Sykes
Tony Hancock*
Tommy Cooper
Danny Kaye*
Phil Silvers*
Robin Williams
Rik Mayall*

These are but a few of my personal favourites* who are diamonds of inspiration, shining on forever.
Oh, and the reason this lose collection of tales are in Freeman's Fables is because, well, if you can't learn from history, when can you learn?

Also by the same author:

Fiction

Freeman's Fables (Vol.1)

Non-Fiction

Belief Nexus
The Time Traveler's Textbook
The Spiritual Pathfinder's Pocketbook

INDEX

There's no more pages, dude. No. No more. Not after this one anyway.

Printed in Poland
by Amazon Fulfillment
Poland Sp. z o.o., Wrocław

63510267R00121